KEEPER OF THE CAPE

Cape Florida

By Kathleen Casper

*To my hundreds of children,
including those from my body and my heart,
as well as those I've cared for and taught.
And all the other future leaders of America.
May we find more pathways that lead us towards
increased understanding and less division. <3*

Keeper of the Cape: Cape Florida

Copyright © 2022 by Kathleen Casper

All rights reserved

No part of this book may be reproduced or transmitted in any form or by any means, electronic or mechanical, including photocopying, recording or by any information storage and retrieval system, without written permission from the author.

Although **Keeper of the Cape: Cape Florida** is based on some historic facts, all characters and locations discussed in the story have been created by the imagination of the author and similarities to any actual people or businesses are merely coincidental.

Printed in the United States of America

Http://OneWorldGifted.weebly.com

Chapter One

They came in droves, floating across the strait in tiny rafts, rowboats, whatever they could find, scattering across the aqua water like seabirds. The panic on their faces told the story of fear and devastation from losing everything as they fled from the Seminoles who were determined to scare off the American settlers who settled along the Miami River.

Men rowed the boats with gusto, waves hitting the bows and spraying the rest of the people who scurried like ants to bail the water out and to keep from losing their belongings that were piled in between their wooden seats. Children cried and their mothers soothed them, trying to keep them still for the rough water crossing. For a bunch of pioneers who were used to toughing the elements, it was clear that those in this crowd were almost to their breaking points.

Charlotte DuBose kept a close eye on the travelers as they approached her side of the crossing. From her vantage point above the beach, standing on the edge of the catwalk around the lighthouse lens she could see if anyone ran into trouble. She knew that within only a few minutes she could make it into her own boat that was hidden in the palm bushes near the keeper house and be on her way into the channel herself.

She worried more about the settlers making it across the water than about the reason they were doing so. She did know a family had been killed down in New River, and it was said that the Seminole Indians were responsible for their deaths. But Charlotte didn't understand the chaos. In her heart she knew she wasn't worried about the local tribe that she had grown up with for the last couple of decades. Her best friend Mica was from the Mayaimi, a branch of that tribe. And Charlotte knew that Mica's family wasn't violent. If anything, Charlotte was terrified for them.

Ever since the Indian Removal Act was approved by Congress, anyone with Native blood was at risk of being kidnapped from their homelands and moved out of the Florida countryside altogether. Rumor had it, they were taking them all the way to some Indian Country by Oklahoma. That was not a journey for the faint of heart either- from what the other settlers were saying, many Indians were dying on that trip, especially those who were young, or old, or sick. And traveling through the wilderness of the Florida Territory was enough to make healthy people sick. Leaving their homes would be hard enough. This land had been their homeland for so many generations.

Charlotte grew up listening to Mica's parents and grandparents tell stories about their life in this lush jungle of land along the edge of the PahayOkee Grassy Waters, or what the Americans called the Everglades.

Mica didn't act scared the last time Charlotte saw her. She swung her shiny black hair away from her cheekbones and laughed, "no one can convince our people to leave our land."

And yet, from what Charlotte's brother, the lighthouse captain was saying from his maritime contacts, the American military was marching into the state in order to forcefully do just that.

"If you need anything…" Charlotte said, choking

back her worries as she hugged her friend goodbye before hiking back down the trail to the keeper's house that she shared with the rest of the DuBose crew, "I will do anything for you."

"I know," Mica stated, smiling her big grin and waving into the air next to her. And then the two friends went their separate ways.

Mica was supposed to be getting married soon. It was rare that the tribe's women could wait until their twenties in order to be matched with a man and expected to settle down and bare children. But Mica was one of the younger "kids" in their large family, so she pretty much had the run of the place and was encouraged to do whatever she wanted, so long as she continued to work hard when they needed her help with fishing and preparing the food.

She had several suitors over the last few years, but her dad prided himself in scaring them away. "No one is good enough for my Mica," he laughed, speaking in a dialect that was a cross between their tribal language and the broken English they had acquired over the last ten years or so since they had negotiated an agreement to share the land with the Americans who had moved into the region.

Charlotte had acquired a strong familiarity with the Mayaimi-English mix and could communicate with just about any tribe that had a similar dialect. And it came in handy when her brother had to talk with the local tribes about maritime things related to boats coming into the Biscayne Bay waterway along the Miami River.

Charlotte remembered the first time she met Mica, when they were only about five years old, and her parents were trying to negotiate a trade with some of the Natives who had some berries and fish for trade along the waterfront. It was one of the first times she had seen the darker-skinned families there, and she was fascinated by the idea of people not speaking English. She and Mica had played in the dirt, quietly tossing rocks around and kicking sticks and smiling at each other.

Their parents finished negotiating, using hand signs and motions, then Charlotte had to leave when they completed the transaction. But she kept begging to go back and play with Mica again and finally her parents relented and started taking her back to the waterfront each week when the tribe women were there to trade their baskets and fish. The friendship grew between their parents, as well as the children. And soon Mica's family was hanging out at the light station with Charlotte's family, and Charlotte's family spent some time at Mica's village several times, too.

Some of the other American settlers criticized the friendship- they felt that the Natives were uncivilized and they shouldn't be talking to them, much less hanging out in their village. But luckily Charlotte's parents disagreed. With only a few-dozen American families in the region, it didn't seem to be an issue if they preferred the company of the Seminoles. Besides, the DuBose family was already seen as outsiders, due to the fact that they didn't move there from the same region of the Northeast as the other Americans. They were already different and hanging out with Mica's family gave them something to do that didn't entail pretending to be more pretentious than they were.

Unfortunately, the one person in her family who seemed to dislike being friendly with the Natives was her brother, Captain Andrew DuBose. Ever since they were young children, her big brother protested having to socialize with Mica's family. He listened more to his teenager peers and believed that it was inappropriate for them to fraternize with the Natives. He also listened to the news that the townsfolk shared from up North, and he knew that the American government believed that Natives should be cleared from the land so that the United States could access more property. It didn't help that at one point her brother had a crush on one of Mica's cousins, who wasn't interested in him... Andrew DuBose was not happy about the Natives being nearby, and he feared that what the government was saying about them was true- that they couldn't be trusted, and that they would kill them in their sleep if they didn't stay alert and guard their families.

Charlotte didn't believe that at all. Mica's tribe was like family to her. But she did worry that the settlers were more likely to harm the tribe out of fear and misinformation.

Now that her brother was the lighthouse keeper instead of her parents and her parents were long-gone, Charlotte felt that if she wasn't there to keep assuring Andrew that the tribe posed no threat, Andrew probably would have already called the military in to rid them of the tribe altogether. Which is what she heard was happening in other areas around the territory.

Charlotte now scanned the water, watching the other terrified settlers scatter across the waves. They were almost to the shore now, so she ran down the stairs in order to go with Andrew and the other townsfolk and their slaves to greet the boats.

She had no idea where they were going to house all of these people. There must be at least thirty boats full of families. That was more than the total of families currently living on the island.

Andrew insisted they could camp in the yard and along the beach if necessary. That it was more important that they vacate their towns along the mainland that the tribes were aware of. Since the Cooley family murders in New River, everyone was afraid they would be victimized next.

Charlotte wasn't completely naïve- she knew there were some renegade natives who were supposedly running wild across the region, burning buildings and destroying crops. They were reacting to the Indian Removal Act, and since they were young enough to have been raised with tribal leaders who were growing wearier of the White people, they didn't have as much restraint as the local tribespeople who were more connected personally with the local settlers.

Plus, right before Charlotte's family had settled in the Cape Florida area from up North, there had been several battles between the American military and the Seminole tribes in Florida. They called those battles the Seminole War now.

Charlotte held an unpopular opinion that she didn't share with others- she didn't think it was the fault of the Seminole that the White people had invaded their lands and tried to kick them out. In the end, the Seminole tribes had agreed to share the land, and things had been pretty peaceful since then.

Now the Americans were reacting out of fear and the unknown, and Charlotte hoped they were wrong. She was looking forward to everyone going back home, so she could continue her normal life along the beautiful island, without so many distractions.

Besides, she was excited about Mica's marriage and maybe even finding someone of her own. But that was a totally different situation. Finding someone who made her feel that way was pretty difficult on the small island. And she was determined not to settle for the first person who made her heart beat quickly.

She glanced across the crowd of landing rowboats and watched several people race to help them.

One of the men who occasionally helped around the lighthouse, John Thompson was working beside her brother. She watched as he reached across a boat to grab a rope and pull a family across the little waves that sprayed them with seafoam. He seemed to be a good man- a little on the quiet side, but he worked hard, and her brother seemed to really like him.

She was intrigued by his glowing blue eyes and the way he stared into hers when he was talking to her, as if she was more important than whatever the topic was. And the way everyone in town flocked to him- even the small kids and animals. It's like they could tell he was one of the kindest people in the area.

She smiled as she watched him hauling the kids out of the rowboat as they clung to his arms, afraid of the waves and not sure where to go while their parents stripped the crates of their only remaining belongings out of the craft and pulling it higher onto the beach. The smaller boy was hanging onto his chest, as he struggled with one arm to move the older boy towards the shore as he kicked through the shallow water.

Charlotte enjoyed watching him juggle the kids, while also admiring his muscular frame. He had his trousers rolled up so they wouldn't get as wet, even though they were getting quite soaked from the splashing water, and she could see his calf muscles tense as he dragged the children through the sand.

John must have sensed her stare, because he glanced her way and smiled at her.

She quickly looked away and found a boat to help with, carrying some of the items from the ship to the shore. It was going to be a long afternoon of settling everyone in around the lighthouse, but seeing John there made it at least a little more entertaining.

John went back to the boat after depositing the children near their mother, and Charlotte continued to watch him as he stole little glimpses of her, too. It was such a hot day, so she blamed that for her pulse increasing but it was sure racing when he looked her way. She wondered if it was obvious to the others on the beach that the two of them kept looking at each other. But no one seemed to be paying attention.

She went over to where the women and children

were gathering and invited them to join her at the keeper house. Everyone needed something, and the women rushed around her to ask her questions about things such as where they could dry off from the water that soaked them during the crossing, or where they should put their things. It was going to be a long day.

Chapter Two

It took over an hour to get all the boats ashore and tied up beyond the high-tide line. And Charlotte and the others hiked each boat load of people up to the keeper's house so they could sit down for a little bit and have some sweet tea to cool off. It was a hot and muggy afternoon, and the bugs were biting. Charlotte was relieved when she was given the job of hostess at the house, so she could get off the hot sand. However, she was not keen on doing a lot of small talk and dealing with emotionally overwrought people was not her favorite thing to do.

The day passed quickly and soon everyone was lounging around the screened porch at the keepers' house. Catharine and a few of the women cooked up some soup that she had started before the boats arrived, and the warm liquid filled everyone's stomachs and calmed their moods.

As night settled in, the settlers pulled whatever blankets and soft clothing they had out of their cases and piled it up around the house. There was barely enough room for walking in between the bedded-down guests, but it would have to do until they could make them all temporary quarters in the yard near the beach.

"We will have a lot of room outside when we make the camp," Andrew assured them.

"This is great," a taller man named Asa said, slapping Andrew's back gently. "We're so glad to have somewhere to stay tonight and friendly faces welcoming us here. Having to leave our homes was very difficult, but this makes it so much better."

Andrew shook his head and shrugged, "I don't really know what we are all going to do, but this is a way we can help each other until we figure it out. And I appreciate having the help with the lighthouse in the meanwhile." He winked, and then invited Asa to join him at daybreak if he wanted to learn how to run a Fresnel lens.

"Anything you need, my friend," Asa smiled, "I would love to learn how it works."

Charlotte could still hear them talking as they walked into the other room to check on all the other guests as they prepared to sleep.

Charlotte gave her bed to one of the families with small children, so she took a space next to her bed on the floor and curled up with a spare blanket and a couple of pillows to cushion her on the wood floor.

She sighed quietly to herself and shivered a little, even though it was more than warm enough. It was sad to think of all the ways that life was going to change at the very least with this latest migration. Having dozens more people to worry about was stressful for the whole family. The DuBose's were used to taking care of themselves, and even though they contributed to community events and helped whenever people needed their help, that was different than having so many homeless friends here all at once. She didn't know what her brother was thinking. Was he looking forward to having these settlers actually settle in on the island, or was he hoping they would move along? She needed to talk with him in the morning.

The thing that worried her the most, was how might these people who were so terrified of Seminoles attacking them impact the relations they currently had with the peaceful tribe at the other end of the island? She knew the hype was spreading and making some folks even more trigger-happy than before. If someone started shooting because they got startled, it could ruin all the years of friendship that her family and others on the island had grown between the Americans and the tribe.

She laid her head on one of the pillows and closed her eyes, watching the shadows from the moonlight outside dance around the little room. It didn't take long before she fell fast asleep.

The house was buzzing with energy as Charlotte came back to consciousness in the morning. She could smell fresh coffee brewing on the woodstove in the main living quarters and she could hear whispering as the guests tried not to wake each other.

She rose, gathering her bedding and shoving it under the bed beside her, and then went outside to the outhouse, pulling her hair into a tie and straightening her skirt and blouse that she hadn't changed out of last night. She knew she looked pretty rough, but she didn't want anyone to think she was being lazy when they all needed so much.

Andrew and Asa were walking back from the light tower and greeted her as she stepped off the porch into the bright sunlight.

"Good morning," she replied, "do you need help with anything?"

"Oh, no," Andrew shook his head and smiled kindly, "Mr. Tift here helped me turn off the light and get the oil hauled up there so it's all set to turn on again this evening."

Charlotte looked at Asa who was grinning from his lighthouse keeper adventure, and she couldn't help but smile back. "You are very helpful, Mr. Tift. Thank you very much. That's a job I sometimes do, and I know the oil can be heavy to haul all the way up those stairs."

She could see Andrew rolling his eyes behind Asa, who was puffing his chest and maybe even tensing his muscles to make himself look even more strong than usual, as he replied, "It was no problem, Ms. Charlotte. No problem at all."

"Well, I hope you have a lot more strength left," Andrew said in a playful tone, "because we have a lot of tent-building to do today to set up everyone's temporary campsites. Charlotte," he turned back to her, "Can you help find all our extra tarps and canvas sheets that we had for making tents and covering the wagon, and then maybe grab some other folks and head into town to see if we could borrow even more from anyone over there? We're going to need an awful lot of tents for all these families."

"Of course," she said. "I will do that right away." She nodded at them both and then continued her journey towards the house to grab her good walking shoes and her handbag.

She saw Catharine shooing some of the older kids into the yard to go play along the beach, and she and a few of the other women were working on making some porridge for breakfast.

"I'm heading into town," Charlotte called to them, "does anyone need anything while I'm there?"

Catharine called back to her, "Can you grab some extra thread from the store? I have some money by the front door in my bag. I will need enough to sew any holes in the tents or blankets that we find as we use up even the ones we thought weren't worth saving. There are so many people, so we will use everything we have."

"I have enough for some thread," Charlotte replied, "I can grab some. Besides, I think we have extra left on our account in town anyway."

Several of the women also offered to help with some money in case they needed anything else, but Charlotte refused to entertain that idea. They would need their money soon enough, as they would soon have to figure out their whole lives if they didn't want to return to their former town.

That must be the worst feeling, she thought to herself, I would never want to just leave and start over. This island has been home for so long, it would be better to risk being killed than to have to leave it at this point.

She waved to the people on the porch as she rushed on by, making sure to not get stuck in conversation, and then walked out to the path behind the house that would take her by the horse corral where her trusty mount, Hershel was housed. If she was going to borrow a bunch of tent material, she would want a horse to help carry it all back.

She found her bay gelding chomping on hay in his enclosure. Aaron must already be somewhere nearby if the horses were eating this early. She watched the horse munch on his breakfast for a little while, then found his bridle and saddlery and tied him up to brush him a bit before saddling up and riding out of the barn area. If she was lucky, the cooler morning air would stick around long enough for them to get into town, and she was counting on the breeze from the trotting horse below her to keep her from sweating horribly in her skirt on the way back. With all of the guests on site that she didn't know very well, she hesitated to throw on a pair of riding chaps like she usually did when riding around the island. It wasn't appropriate for women to dress like men, but the island was like another world when it came to rules and procedures. No one ever said anything about her unconventional gear, and they certainly would never complain to Captain DuBose, who would laugh them right off the island. Living as settlers in the Florida Territory definitely had its perks!

As she rounded a bend in the road she came upon a small hole in the otherwise thick bushes. This was where she and Mica used to part ways when Mica walked her back to the lighthouse property. She felt a lump in her throat as she thought of the cheerful face that she last saw departing through the thicket there just weeks ago.

She wondered if Mica was afraid to come over to visit now that the settlers were camping all over the place. If Mica wore some of the clothing she had borrowed from Charlotte over the years and put her hair up into a bonnet, she might pass for a European-American settler for long enough to make it through the camp areas. But maybe Mica wasn't as aware of how predisposed the settlers were with their own business. She probably worried she would be harassed, or even harmed.

That made Charlotte feel terrible. Her friend was more welcome at her home than any of those strangers. Hopefully they would be able to figure out how to all live peacefully again soon.

She continued riding towards town and soon found small buildings lining the muddy road and people bustling about from wooden building to building. It wasn't a large town by any means- mostly consisting of the trading goods general store, the little saloon on the corner, a tailor, a butcher shop, and the shoemaker. Small homes lined another couple of small roads behind Main Street, and small boats lined the little harbor along the bay.

Tying the horse to one of the hitches, she made her

way into the general store and looked around the rows of shelves to where she could see Mr. Henderson sweeping the floor near the main counter.

"Hello, Ms. DuBose," he said, inviting her in. "What can I do for you today?"

"Hello, Mr. Henderson. I need to buy this thread," she said, picking some up off the counter. "Also, my brother was hoping you could help us with loaning us some of your extra tents or tarps. We need to house a lot of people right now," she started to explain.

But he cut her off, "I know about the guests," he said. "I was down at the beach helping for a bit as they all came in on their boats. I told Captain DuBose I would be happy to help by loaning him all the tarps and canvases I have. Just sit still and I will go grab them and help you with them."

He stepped towards the back door to go into his storage area, then paused. "How are you supposed to get all those tarps back to your home?"

"I brought my horse," she laughed. "I certainly couldn't carry them on my own."

He smiled in relief, "Alright, but I still don't know if you can take them all at one time."

"I will sure try, though," she said, "We definitely need them as soon as possible."

"How about if I send one of my workers with you?" he offered. "I have Rem, the kid who always helps around here, and he can take my horse with you so you can take twice as many tarps."

Charlotte knew Rem, as he was one of Mica's cousins who often helped around town and was always cheerful and happy to assist with all sorts of jobs.

"Rem is still working here?" She asked, surprised.

"Yes, but we are keeping that kind of quiet. I will give him one of my hats to wear and instruct him not to go all the way to where everyone is camping. He said he still needs some things before his family moves to somewhere safer so he wants to work just a little more."

She was impressed with Rem's desire to keep working. A lot of the people staying at Charlotte's house said some pretty bad things about the Seminoles- that they were lazy and wanted to steal from the Americans. But from what she had seen all these years, they were some of the hardest-working people she knew.

She eagerly waited for Mr. Henderson to fetch Rem from the back of the store.

When Rem followed Mr. Henderson out of the back room, they both had their arms full of tarps and blankets.

"I found some blankets to send along, too. I'm sure they can use them," he said.

She nodded, then ran up to Rem to help him with part of his stack. "I'm so glad to see you are doing ok," she whispered to him.

He nodded, smiling up at her with his big brown eyes, under the big hat he was borrowing from Mr. Henderson, then the two of them loaded them onto Hershel and Mr. Henderson's pinto pony that he led to the front of the store.

They made their way along the road, balancing all the tarps. When they got back to the light station, Rem helped unload the tents by the entrance to the property, but he wouldn't go any further.

"Thank you, Rem," she smiled at him.

He didn't smile back, but he tipped his head and rode away on his pony.

Charlotte wanted to ask him about Mica and his family. But he didn't seem very talkative. She decided she would find a way to slip back out at some point and go find Mica. She started hauling the tarps towards the cottage. Andrew and Mr. Tift saw her approaching and called to others to help her.

Eventually they had the tents and tarps ready for the families to sleep in and Charlotte snuck off to take some time for herself before dinner.

Chapter Three

The Miami guests were getting restless. After just a couple of days of camping on the island, they were tired of dealing with the sand fleas and the no-see-um bugs that attacked them relentlessly every evening. And they were ready to find somewhere to settle permanently.

"We could just stay here," Andrew insisted, "we have just about anything we need here. The town has a good trading post ,and the military is always patrolling along this coast. We are as safe as we would be anywhere else."

Two dozen families were crammed into the small space on the keeper's screened porch. It was getting late and after a filling dinner of salted pork and fresh salad from the garden, Charlotte knew they must all be getting ready to settle in for the night. But at first it seemed to be a fun party, with someone playing a fiddle and everyone else joining in to sing along with the old favorites.

But, as the sun set, their anxiety set in as well. Darkness seemed to accentuate the fear of the unknown and remind them of having to return to their make-shift tents of canvas sheets on wooden frames, strung between the bushes on the edge of the shore. There was nothing cozy about their situation, and Charlotte couldn't blame them for wanting to find somewhere else to live.

"We can't stay in tents much longer," one of the men with a long beard and a gruff voice spoke softly and the rest of the group nodded and mumbled support.

He went on, "We sure appreciate your hospitality, Captain DuBose and Miss DuBose. But, we need to find somewhere to live that we can actually settle in. This island is beautiful, and we appreciate everything you have done to help us feel welcome. Yet, we all know this island is still at-risk for Indian attack. And we need to find somewhere that we can work and provide for our families better than on the island."

Michael Carson jumped in, "We definitely are thankful to the DuBose family," he said, hugging his young and obviously pregnant wife closer to his side and looking at her momentarily. She nodded and smiled encouragement, then he continued, "But when we walked into town the other day, we heard that everyone else is heading down to Key West. Apparently, the town there is safe from attacks because they have the Army stationed at the entrance to town and no one can get in or out without them knowing about it. They have a lot of rations there, and ships are docking down there to provide even more trade opportunities. They are fishing and not afraid of being seen from the shores by Seminoles."

Another man agreed and added more information, saying, "A lot of people are heading down there now, and we plan to join them. If we leave in a few days, we can join the big caravan that's heading south. It's really the only way we can be assured of safety, and with my wife, Leila expecting again, we just can't risk being somewhere unsafe right now."

"We also plan to join them," Michael said, "and I hope you all will come along, too."

Others also chimed in, saying they also wanted to join the caravan.

Charlotte knew they weren't comfortable in the tents, but she worried that Andrew would listen to this fearmongering and want to leave, too. She couldn't imagine actually having to move. This was their home, and Andrew had been appointed by the Lighthouse Service to stay at the post until he was discharged officially. She sure hoped he would let them all go, but he would stay here. There was nothing to worry about, so leaving seemed riskier than staying at that point.

She left the porch to go inside. It was going to be a long night with all those people getting riled up about moving, but she would rather do some reading by candlelight and then get some extra sleep. The discussion was making her stress more than she wanted to. If those folks wanted to head down to the Keys, they should do that. But Charlotte didn't plan on going anywhere.

Chapter Four

The preparations for making everyone comfortable and setting up the campsites kept everyone busy enough that Charlotte was able to slip away unnoticed. She found Aaron in the back of the keeper's cottage cutting some wood for the fireplace so the townsfolk could continue cooking and preserving foods for the trip.

"Are you worried about this moving idea?" She asked him when she was standing across the wood pile from his chopping block.

He paused momentarily and looked at her. She saw him start to shrug, then stop and just look at her with a defeated look. "I think things will get way worse for everyone if we go. But I don't think staying here alone is a good option for your family either."

Charlotte nodded. "I don't care about us... I'm worried about you. What will it be like down in the Keys if people are already treating you so badly here on Key

Biscayne?"

This time he shrugged all the way, letting his shoulders drop back into place and swinging the ax again, splitting the pine wood in two large pieces. "I will be fine, Miss DuBose."

"Quit that Miss DuBose stuff," Charlotte tensed, realizing he was more upset about the week's events than she expected. "You know you don't have to do that with me."

He shrugged and glanced at the road behind her, avoiding her stare. He seemed on-edge and constantly worried that someone might not think he was properly in "his place." That made Charlotte feel sick inside. Aaron was one of her favorite people in the world and he didn't deserve to worry like that.

"Look, Aaron, I don't intend to go down to the Keys with all those rude and uppity people. I want to stay with the lighthouse and try to find Mica and her family so I can help them if more military troops really are coming to capture them all."

Their eyes locked again before he split the next piece. "I don't think you should stay here," he said softly. "It's not safe for a single woman. I see how those men from Miami look at you. And those are the ones who have social reasons to treat you respectfully. What will happen when you are alone and some of those renegade guys who are out hunting the Seminole come along and find you here? Or what about the little groups of Seminoles who are burning camps and killing settlers?"

Charlotte shivered inside a little at those ideas. But she was more worried about Mica than herself. Plus, someone had to keep the light running. And she didn't think their little island would be as much of a target as the larger civilizations.

"I will be fine," she said, "I know how to take care of myself."

He nodded, "I know you can. You are the strongest woman I know here. But I don't think being here alone is ok." He kicked some sand with his toe as he leaned the ax down and then quietly said, "maybe I can stay too."

She grabbed a prickly piece of wood that had split from his last swing and piled it up with the others in the small lean-to shed. She smiled up at him. "I would love it if you could stay. But I doubt Andrew will want you stay here. They probably need you."

"I hate to think of them needing me, but I'd feel

worse leaving you here alone and needing me, too."

"Well, it would be your choice, I'm sure," Charlotte agreed. Even though most Americans had issues with Black people having any choices, she was glad that Andrew didn't think of Aaron as a slave. Florida Territory was different than the states- there was no expectation that all dark-skinned people were to be owned by other people. They even made a new law that protected Florida as a non-slave territory recently.

There were some families who moved down to Florida with their slaves from up North, and they kept them and treated them like slaves regardless of the new law. However, several former slaves had escaped from northern states and were living free in areas across Florida. Andrew always had insisted on paying Aaron for his work anyway, but Aaron helped way more than what he was compensated for, which made Charlotte uncomfortable.

Charlotte heard that men from the north were coming down to Florida in order to capture those former slaves and haul them back to the northern regions so they could make money on them. But Andrew wasn't like that, and he would never have permitted such a thing happen to Aaron. He may not have always agreed with Charlotte about the Seminole issues, but he did not think of Aaron as a slave. Maybe that was because of his position with the Lighthouse Service being well-paid and respected, and he handled his work just fine without help. Likely it was because Aaron Carter had come along and offered to help around the light station out of his interest in nautical things and his desire to find work.

"I respect a hard-working man, and Aaron works really hard," Andrew once told Charlotte when she asked him about it. "I don't care to get involved with the politics of the North. I like things down here because they are simple, and we aren't under as many rules from the government here. Why would I want to start catering to their notions of what's right and what's wrong, when I get about my business here just fine?"

Charlotte was glad to have Aaron around, because often he filled in on things so Andrew could do more things with his children. His ten-year-old daughter, Margaret and seven-year-old son, Fred would otherwise run wild all over the island, and Charlotte was not one to want to be a nursemaid to kids.

They also enjoyed knowing that the Lighthouse

Service considered it a well-run station and the officers didn't often bother them because their inspections were always top-notch. A lot of that was because Aaron and Andrew both worked on keeping everything running smoothly. That gave her, and Andrew's wife, Catharine time to do the cooking and salting the meats and keeping the house in decent order for all of them. Having everyone pitching in sure helped for an orderly household.

"I don't want to take you away from helping Andrew's family if it means they are at more risk of harm during their journey," Charlotte admitted to Aaron.

He was done chopping wood and the pieces were stacked, so he leaned against the shed in the shade and wiped the sweat from his forehead. August in southern Florida Territory was brutally hot and humid. Even though they had a cooler front blow through, the sun seemed to bake everything under it, even through the grey clouds.

"Don't worry so much, Charlotte," Aaron grinned. "You always worry. I think your brother and all those know-it-all men from Miami will figure things out just fine."

Charlotte laughed. He was right, the way those men carried about, saying so much about everything, they had better know what they were doing. She would go with them herself if she really thought they needed help. It was likely that they would get down to Key West after the crazy-long journey and get an extended vacation with the rest of the Americans who were running there for safety. And in the end, nothing would probably even happen here, so they would be back soon anyway.

"I need to figure out where Mica and her family are," Charlotte said. "I have a feeling they are the ones we should be more worried about."

Aaron nodded, "I don't know what I'm more worried about… their Mayaimi tribe being safe, or us being safe from the rebel Indians who are rumored to be burning villages to protest the Indian Removal Act," he said.

Charlotte knew better than to be surprised at how aware Aaron was about the news. He often was the one who brought them information from town, as sometimes being isolated on the tip of the Key Biscayne island meant being the last people to know about local gossip. However, when the Lighthouse Service sent them news or the people in town running the telegraph shared information with them, Andrew made sure Aaron was the one who took it to the community, so there was reciprocal information trade happening. If they shared their news, they knew others would be happy to keep them informed as well.

"I hope the rebels stay away," Charlotte agreed, "but I also hope the military will keep their distance, and that the northern slave hunters stay away too."

Aaron looked at her with a serious look, brushing away some of the tiny "no-see-um" flies that were taking advantage of the sweet sweat on his brow. "I agree with that."

"But you're safe here with us, Aaron Carter," she smiled and patted his arm. "I would fight to the death to keep you from being taken up north."

Aaron smiled back. "I will be okay, Charlotte. But at least we have those papers, just in case…"

He was referring to the paperwork that Andrew insisted on drafting after Aaron had worked with them a year or two. They said that Aaron was the property of Captain Andrew DuBose, and they had one of their friends who was a local sheriff sign them as a witness, and then they even had the local governmental office seal them with wax for the sake of making them extra-official.

Aaron trusted that Andrew would never use those papers against him, but they should keep him safe in case anyone from up north came around looking for rebellious former slaves.

That seemed great and all, but Charlotte wondered if they would really matter if what Aaron had hinted at before was true. When he claimed to have escaped from the north in a hurry when he was just a boy, and he thought maybe someone might be missing him. As long as whoever came around didn't have Aaron on their specific list, he should be okay. At least, she hoped so.

That was one reason why she didn't want to risk having him stick around the lighthouse, in case someone did happen to come by and double check everyone's identifications. It hadn't been an issue for the last ten years or so, but now that so many people were worried about cleaning out Florida so it could possibly be a new state, like what the governor kept hinting at, they may be checking more documents than before.

"Don't worry about any of that now. It's not

something we can control. Let's go see what kind of chaos is ensuing inside," Aaron grinned and motioned towards the house where dozens of guests were milling about on the porches and inside.

They each picked up a few smaller pieces of wood to stock the fire, and then walked towards the back door and all of the noise.

Chapter Five

Inside, children ran in between the chairs where some of the older men and women sat, cooling themselves with handheld fans. Some of the younger women were cooking pots of porridge and other dishes that could be contained without spoiling for the long trip. And Charlotte could see some of the women out in the side yard rubbing salt into the carcasses of pigs and fowl that the men brought to them for preservation.

"Charlotte!" she heard someone calling to her from the front porch. She looked towards the screened room and could make out the shape of her sister-in-law, Catharine motioning for her to join her out there.

"Charlotte, do you know where Andrew keeps the small tool set for working on the lighthouse?" She asked. "We have one pig with a very stubborn slug in it."

Charlotte raised an eyebrow as she asked, "a slug? As in, a bullet? Why would anyone have to kill a pig with a bullet around here? Seems our pigs are tamer than any pet dog."

"Apparently some of these Miami boys enjoy playing with guns since they don't get as many opportunities in town where they can just buy their own meat. Andrew must have let him shoot one for the fun of it, but now it's not going to be as appetizing with a bullet inside. We need the tools so we can pry the bullet out from between some bone fragments."

Charlotte sighed, she hated any type of suffering, and figured that hanging the pig was a much more humane way to kill it, rather than shooting it without knowing for sure if it would die immediately or not. She shook her head; those town folks were going to cause way too many problems. She wished they would just go back home.

"I will go get the tools," Charlotte agreed, then walked through the other people who were congregated on the porch, enjoying the little bit of a breeze that blew through their many hot and sweaty bodies. The tools were probably at the base of the lighthouse, as Andrew and Aaron used them for all sorts of repairs.

Charlotte liked that she was the one who Catharine

asked to retrieve them, because it illustrated that Charlotte was almost like one of the men in terms of her engagement with the actual lighthouse projects. She often helped the two men with tasks because she was interested in knowing how things work, and because they knew she understood the operations just as well as they did. Her dad often had her help around their Florida property when she was a kid, and although Andrew eventually was chosen to be the lighthouse keeper for the island by the Lighthouse Service, everyone knew Charlotte was the one with the strongest mechanical understanding. Sometimes she wondered if that was why Andrew let her stay on the lighthouse property with his family, even more than just to help his wife with the cooking and the kids.

As she rounded the side of the brick and cement structure, she was startled to see someone else standing there in the shade.

"Charlotte," the figure said, moving towards her.

She stepped back in surprise, but then relaxed as she recognized the solid shape of John Thompson.

"What are you doing over here?" She asked, trying to detract from her obviously unsettled reaction.

"Andrew asked me to come out here to check and see if the Carson family was doing ok. They hadn't come over to help this morning and he was thinking maybe something was wrong or that maybe they left already- they were the ones who wanted to head out to Key West right away."

Charlotte's eyes widened at the idea of settlers already heading out. She also couldn't help but think about how much she loved the way John spoke. He was from Delaware, and he didn't have the southern drawl like so many of the people in Florida who came from Virginia and the southern states. His voice was clear and precise, and it matched his matter-of-fact nature.

"Oh," Charlotte said, "are they okay?"

He shrugged, "I couldn't find them. I think they probably went into town instead of hanging out here. I don't think they actually left yet. But I will check on them again later, just in case they need anything. There weren't any signs of trouble in their camp area." He paused, then asked, "What are you doing here, Ms. Charlotte?"

"I'm supposed to be retrieving some tools. Catharine said one of the Miami boys shot one of the pigs and they need something to get the bullet out with."

She watched as John's shoulders moved as he laughed with her. They tapered down nicely to his waist, with his muscular chest somewhat hidden in his shirt- another example of strength that wasn't boastful but was just there. Like his stoic confidence.

"I can help you get the tools, if it means getting some extra time with you," he smiled at her.

She felt her cheeks blush and she stared him right back in the eyes to show him she was not one of the other women who might cave against some flattery. "Thanks, but I can get them myself."

"I know you can," he said slowly, "but I would be honored if you let me join you. Besides," he smiled again, "you are much better company than all those Miami boys."

Charlotte couldn't help but smile back. He was one of her favorite people on the island, but she sure didn't want him to know it. She saw how silly the other women got when men were around, and she refused to give anyone that kind of power over her.

"Ok, John Thompson," she nodded, "you can come with me. Just don't touch anything- you might break something."

She could hear him laughing behind her as she continued around the side of the lighthouse to the doorway, and she found the hidden key next to the door jamb and let them inside.

The cool air from inside the solid structure felt amazing on her skin, and she closed the door behind them quickly so it wouldn't heat up right away.

"Mmmm," she sighed, "I love it in here on hot days."

She could see John nod in the shadowy room. A ray of sunlight trickled down from the window on the stairway landing way above and a little light peeked through the cracks around the door, but it was mostly dark with the door closed.

"I hope you don't mind that I love being in here with you," John said slowly with his gruff voice as he stared her deep in the eyes.

Charlotte felt something jump inside her chest. The electricity between them in this closed space was much more noticeable than she expected. She froze in place and tried to come up with something witty to say in response.

But then she felt his hand on hers, and she felt him tug on it a little bit. Her will power was limited for some reason, and she felt herself moving towards him in the dark room.

He raised her arm a little and it stopped her from leaning against his chest, like she was about to do with the momentum behind his tug and her lack of force against it. She felt his warm breath against her hand, as he raised it to his lips and brushed them across it. "I couldn't possibly pass up this opportunity to kiss you, Miss Charlotte DuBose," he whispered.

She felt the goosebumps rise on the backs of her arms, as the electricity coursed through them. She pulled her arm back, slowly. "Mr. John Thompson," she said, realizing her voice sounded a little less than solid as she stepped back, "I don't know what you are doing with me…"

She saw his smile, even through the shadows. "I don't know what you are doing with me," he replied, grinning at her wavering voice. "But, we better find those tools."

She wasn't sure if she was disappointed by his restraint, or if she was thankful. She was attracted to so many things about him, but she also didn't want anyone to think she was weak. And she certainly didn't want anyone else on the island or anywhere to ever think she was being improper with a man. Especially when she had more important things to worry about.

"Yes," she said, moving towards the area under the stairs where she knew Andrew kept them. "I think you were trying to distract me."

"Of course, I would never do anything like that," he said, chuckling.

Charlotte gave him a stern look and then shoved a big wooden box into his arms. "I assume you came in here with me so you could help this poor little woman carry that big box of tools…?"

He laughed again and nodded, "I would be happy to do that," he said. "Although, that wasn't exactly why I came with you."

"I know," Charlotte said, trying not to laugh with him. She shook her head, "I don't know what I'm going to do with you, John Thompson. But I do know we better get that box to Catharine before she starts worrying that I've been captured by Indians."

They smiled at each other, and Charlotte tried to

regain her composure as she pushed the door back open. As they walked out into the blinding sunshine she locked the door behind them, then scuffled her feet across the dirt path as she rushed to walk ahead of him so he couldn't see her cheeks still burning.

Chapter Six

The boats were loaded up and some already were crossing Biscayne Bay as Charlotte stood on the catwalk next to the Fresnel lens in the top of the lighthouse. This time she watched for any sign of distress from her brother's boat, feeling a sense of dread in his departure. It was nice to have the whole place to herself, she half-smiled. But, the journey they were taking was not without risk, and she was going to miss those silly kids and Catharine. And even though her brother was sometimes a little overbearing, she would worry a lot about Andrew too.

He didn't like her staying behind. He refused at first, saying she would be easy prey for anyone who wanted to take advantage of a lone woman. But she promised she would hide, other than taking care to make sure the light stayed bright each night. They argued for a long time, but Andrew knew his sister well. He wasn't going to win, and even if he hogtied her and threw her in the boat, she would find a way to return if she had that in her mind as what she was hellbent on doing. So, he finally gave in and said he would return for her after taking his family across the channel and making sure everyone else got across and settled into their journey. Charlotte assured him she would be fine until he could make it back and agreed to be ready in a few weeks for that return once his family was safe and he could chance such a trip.

Aaron volunteered to stay with Charlotte so she at least had someone nearby if she ran into trouble. She was not thrilled with having anyone babysit her, but Aaron was one of her favorite people and she hoped he would be safer staying than going anywhere with that large group of white strangers. Andrew reluctantly let Aaron stay. He knew Aaron knew the property better than anyone. And he also knew Aaron would protect Charlotte from danger.

The other town folk would not like that Charlotte was staying behind for long. Andrew had to lie and say that she and Aaron were going to catch up with the last bit of supplies after they secured the lighthouse. It was unlikely anyone would notice their longer absence for a while, and by then Andrew would be on his way back to pick them up anyway.

Andrew's boat entered the current about halfway into their mini regatta. He wanted to make sure those families who needed extra assistance had help first, but he also didn't want to send everyone off without him if there was any chance of danger. That came from his seafaring days when he was captain of ships and had to be responsible for anything that could happen. Charlotte imagined he still thought of himself as a real captain, even though he was of a lighthouse that was not sailing anywhere now.

She saw the two kids shading their eyes to find her in the treetops as the tip of the lighthouse came into their view. They waved with more energy than Charlotte could muster in her response wave. She blew them kisses and her niece blew them right back as they waved and laughed in the ocean spray.

She watched as the rest of the boats charged into the water and then kept her eyes on their glistening forms as they made the long crossing and then disappeared into the harbor beyond her line of sight.

She sighed and turned towards the staircase to escape into the top of the lighthouse for some solitude and time to sort her thoughts about the work ahead.

But just as she was about to step onto the first stair, she saw a shape out of the corner of her eye, walking towards the tower below her. She knew Aaron was at his cabin and would not be back anytime soon so no one else should be near the light station.

She spun around and her body tensed a little more than she expected. She didn't like the idea of being jumpy now that she had to be strong and on her own, but she knew there was always a chance that someone could target the lighthouse if they believed it was abandoned.

She squinted her eyes and glanced below, stooping down so whoever it was couldn't see her as easily. She could see a shape entering the door below. She crept as quietly as possible down the first flight and hid behind the little hatch door that led to the next level of stairs.

She could hear someone climbing below her, and realized she had nothing to protect herself with. She froze in the shadows, prepared to use the weight of her body to push whoever it was back down the stairs.

Just as the person reached the other side of the little doorway, a familiar voice called out, "Charlotte? Charlotte it's me, John."

She dropped her arms from their position on the back of the door and relaxed her pose. "John Thompson, what the hell are you doing here?"

She slowly opened the hatch so he wouldn't get knocked down, even though part of her was so embarrassed by her nervous reaction that she almost wanted to see that happen.

Why was that man still here? She didn't know whether to be happy to see him, because she really enjoyed his company, or mad that he was ruining her mini vacation from humans.

"I decided to stay behind and help you gather up the supplies so you could rejoin the others quicker. I didn't like the idea of you being left behind."

Charlotte shook her head. There was no harm now in alerting him to the real plan. "I wasn't really going to try to catch up with them," she admitted. "I was staying to keep the light going. Andrew wanted me to join everyone later, and he planned to come back. But I was hoping to show him by then that I was safe, and everything was fine, so we didn't have to abandon our home."

John sighed. "I had a feeling you were up to something like that," he said. "That's another reason I stayed behind. I didn't want to think of what could happen to you if I just left too."

If ever she had believed she needed a man like John, all hope went out the door at that point. He was just like the others, wanting to control what she did and believing she couldn't do it without a man helping her. Ugh. She turned away from him and started wiping the Fresnel lens to ready it for the night.

John grabbed one of the other cloths from the bucket and started shining the glass next to her.

Charlotte tried to ignore him for a few minutes, but then couldn't contain herself anymore. "Why do men always think women need so much help with everything?" she burst out, glaring at him when he looked up in surprise.

"I don't think you need help, Charlotte," he finally said in a low voice. "I think you are one of the strongest women I know… strongest people I know…"

"Then why didn't you just figure I would be fine staying here for a while and go on your way with all the other men?" She didn't want to let down her guard and give him any indication that somewhere behind her frustration she was actually pleased to know he felt that way about her. She was even more determined to be tough so he wouldn't see the weakness that even being next to him caused her to enjoy the situation more than her gruff exterior let on.

"I think the problem was that I wouldn't be okay worrying about you from afar," he said, putting his rag down to get more soapy water. "I couldn't live with not knowing what happened to you if I never saw you again."

Charlotte scoffed, "not every woman needs a man to worry about her."

"I know," he said, half-smiling, "but I can't help but want you to be okay."

"Hmph," she didn't know what else to say. There was plenty of work to get done and she didn't have time to argue with him. Plus, he could definitely help with the tasks so she could concentrate on finding out more about

Mica and her tribe. She wanted to make sure they were okay and to find out what she could do to help.

Just then, Aaron came around the bend under the tower and Charlotte waved him up. He climbed up to the top and poked his head in the small room. "Where did he come from?" he pointed at John, surprised to see additional feet behind the lens.

"He apparently didn't think I was going to be okay by myself. Even though I wasn't even as by myself as it seemed," she said, rolling her eyes.

"Hi Aaron," John smiled. "I am here to help the two of you with whatever needs to be done."

Aaron laughed, "I always thought you were a little crazy, but this takes the cake! Why wouldn't you have gone with the others to find a safer location?"

John shrugged, "well, I'm hoping this place will be safe enough. Besides, I figured you could use another hand."

"We definitely could use more help, that's for sure," Aaron smiled. "Thank you for risking your life to help us."

John nodded, "thank you for not chasing me out of here," he looked directly at Charlotte who pretended to not be paying attention.

"I was thinking I might go take a walk around the perimeter of the town to see what everyone left behind and to make sure that the place is nice and quiet. If anyone was watching before, this would be the time they might try to break into camp and mess with everything."

John nodded, "I imagine you're right. I will help finish up the lighthouse tasks but let me know when you get back if you need me to help with anything. We likely will need to secure the access roads, so we know if anyone ever does come by."

Aaron agreed and then headed down the stairs and out of the tower. Charlotte could see his khaki shirt disappear around the bend in the path near the tree line.

"I really don't mean to upset you," John said softly towards Charlotte as they continued to polish the windows and lens panels.

Charlotte only nodded his way and continued the circular motion on the glass.

Chapter Seven

Aaron returned after several hours with tales about all the things left behind in the rush of the townsfolks' retreat. "We have plenty of supplies in town," he assured them. "Pretty much anything we need."

They all sat around the dining room table in the keeper house, taking a break from the day's work.

"How did it look in terms of safety?" John asked. "Was there any sign of anyone else being left behind or coming into town after they left?"

"I didn't see anything out of the ordinary," Aaron said. "I was disheartened to see so much livestock left though. So many animals and they certainly can't take care of themselves."

"Maybe the Mayaimi Seminole tribe will want them," Charlotte suggested. "I could run over there and ask if they would like to take whatever we can't use ourselves."

"I'm not sure that's a good idea," John started to say.

But then Aaron cut him off, looking a bit sheepish for being disrespectful, but also acknowledging Charlotte's attachment to her neighbors and friends. "It's a good idea," he said, looking directly at Charlotte so not to chance a dirty look from John.

But John, so far, was sitting respectfully across the table and listening to Aaron. Perhaps, Charlotte thought, John realized that he was now the guest in a different social caste. Either that, or he was like Andrew, respectful of people no matter their race when no one who cared was around. She hoped for the latter.

"I'm just concerned that someone else may be out there in the woods along your way," Aaron continued. "I think we should scout things out a bit more before you chance it."

Charlotte nodded and smiled. Aaron could have run off by now if he wanted to be freer than what her family offered him. She almost wanted that for him, but she realized that there was security in knowing he had access to supplies and shelter. She wondered if he would eventually decide to go. She wouldn't try to stop him. Sometimes she could tell he was thinking about faraway places and people, and she wished she could give that all to him. It was a hard world to live in for a woman, with men trying to tell her what to do and expecting certain behaviors from her all the time. But she knew it was even harder for Aaron and other Black people. And she knew how much worse it would be if the wrong people found him.

"Thank you, Aaron," she said, reaching out to his hand.

He took hers in his and squeezed it. He didn't say anything else, and she didn't elaborate. But they both knew what the other was thinking.

She watched John look away from them briefly, with a slight flush of his cheeks. Was he really jealous of what he just saw between her and Aaron? She hid her smile, wondering what else she could do to make him squirm a little. Besides, she didn't mind Aaron's touch. Even though she knew Andrew would have called her out on being inappropriate, and other men might have hurt Aaron for braving to touch a white woman. But no one else was there and John didn't seem to want to get involved in any drama.

There was always something calming about Aaron that she craved. If things were different and they weren't living such separate lives even in the same camp, she would love to have a man who was as capable and brilliant as Aaron.

She stood up and walked to the window and peered out into the dark shadows that were collecting under the trees. "I will need to light the lamp soon," she said, pointing to the light tower above them. They both nodded.

John stood up, "I'm going to bed down in here," he said, pointing to the living room just beyond the dining area, "If you don't mind. I want to make sure we stay close together since there are only a few of us here."

Aaron nodded, "I think that's a good plan. Are you okay with that Charlotte?"

She didn't even hesitate, "of course. I think you both should stay here. We have plenty of room and you both are familiar with the accommodations."

Aaron stared at her. "I can't stay in your house," he said. "If anyone saw me staying in the home of a white lady, I would be shot on sight."

"Good thing no one else is here," John said, smiling. "I'm fine with you staying here too. It would be better to have two of us here if anything did happen."

"I don't know…" Aaron started to argue.

Charlotte stood up abruptly. "Of course, you have to stay here, Aaron Carter. Don't even think another thing of it. We have supplies for an army in this cellar and we have enough work to keep several people busy. I would be honored to have you stay with us." She didn't want to chance anything dangerous happening- either from outside the house or within it, if she was left with John Thompson and no one else to chaperone. The thought of what she would do if John tried to kiss another part of her body made her weak, and she certainly didn't like feeling that way in any circumstance.

Aaron finally relented and went to gather his bedding and other belongings for the evening. Which indeed left her alone with John temporarily.

"You know I could have kept you safe without Aaron," John whispered as Aaron was exiting the porch and heading across the yard to his cabin.

"I don't know how safe I would be with you, Mr. Thompson," she quipped, and then regretted the words as soon as they left her mouth.

"Oh really?" John's eyes widened and his soft mouth turned up in the corners. "Am I dangerous for you, Miss DuBose?" he grinned.

"I don't know what to think of you, Mr. Thompson. Are you dangerous?" she asked, avoiding his gaze.

"I would never let anything happen to you…. that you didn't want to happen," he said. "But yes, I could be dangerous."

With that, Charlotte spun around and walked out of the room to find him some bedding and to get away from the heat that was enveloping her when she was near him. She fanned herself when she was out of his view and could tell he was in the other room chuckling. Why did she let him get to her like that? He wasn't even supposed to be there at all. And here they were, trying to keep the town and the lighthouse secure and instead she was getting all flustered from some silly flirtation. She promised herself this would not keep happening. Besides, Aaron would be disappointed in her inability to keep her head, and she didn't want to make him uncomfortable. It did help having two men there. Otherwise, she would likely get herself into some compromising situations if she was left with one man there to give her undivided attention. Apparently, she was weaker than she thought she was, and that made her quite disappointed. She would keep her head, no matter what.

She grabbed the blankets and a down pillow and returned to the living area where she tossed the stack next to John and without looking at him left to go light the flame in the lens.

She could tell John was staring at her the whole time, but she would not give him the satisfaction of even acting like she knew he was there.

Chapter Eight

When Charlotte returned to the keeper house after her lighthouse duties, she found the men at the table, discussing some safety issues.

"We need to make sure we have decent water," Aaron explained to her. "It's possible that our water supply could be tainted if there truly are rogue Natives running around trying to harm white people right now."

"I don't think anyone would bother to do that to harm just the three of us," Charlotte replied.

"No one would know it was just us here," John reminded her. "For all anyone else knows, this town is still in full operation and everyone is still here. And that big lighthouse of yours is certainly a beacon of civilization so we would be quick targets of inhospitality if anyone would want to harm us."

"I'm not going to darken the light," Charlotte said, looking quickly at both men. "We have to keep it lit. It's our job. And if anyone is trying to get here as a refugee, we have to make sure they don't crash on all the rocks."

The men exchanged a knowing glance.

"It's going to make targets of us, that's all," Aaron said. "I know how you feel about the light staying lit. But that just means we have to make sure our water is safe and that we know who is coming along the roads."

She nodded. "I think we are safe tonight. I didn't see any sign of activity anywhere nearby when I looked out from the tower. Can we at least try to get some sleep?"

They agreed it was late and they were all going to need more energy the following day. The men retreated to their blankets on the couches in the living room and Charlotte went upstairs to her bed.

It felt strange to only have two men in the house with her instead of all the other people who had congregated there for days prior to their departure to Key West. But it was nice to not be one of the people traveling right now. Being in her comfortable and familiar bed seemed absolutely luxurious. She blew out her lantern and cuddled up under the sheets until sleep came.

The next morning, she woke to a strange silence. Mornings usually were filled with voices from townsfolk stopping by, the screams and laughter of children and the hustle and bustle of Andrew and his family tending to the horses and cattle. But it was eerily quiet without all of that.

She wandered down to check on Aaron and John, but they were already up and outside somewhere. She got herself ready for the day quickly and started to warm up a pan to cook some eggs and bacon for breakfast.

Aaron came into the kitchen first, apologizing for just walking in. "I don't mean to impose, Charlotte," he said, "but I did smell the bacon!"

She laughed, "set the table then, and we will eat some of it shortly."

She watched him move around the room, smiling at his cheerful demeanor. We could be in the middle of a war and Aaron would probably find the silver lining, she thought. She was glad he was the one who offered to stick around with her. She loved her brother dearly, but having someone much more cheerful around was a breath of fresh air.

She sensed John watching her from the doorway before she heard his voice. She looked past Aaron and felt her breath catch in her throat for a minute when she saw him there without a shirt on.

"I'm sorry, Charlotte," he said, reaching for his shirt on one of the chairs inside the door. "I meant to bring my shirt with me, but I decided to jump in the shower for a minute. I was pretty sweaty after running back to my house to check on things this morning."

Charlotte smiled politely and pretended not to be affected by his chiseled chest as he threw the shirt over his head and meandered into the room. He sat in one of the chairs and nodded at Aaron who handed him some silverware.

"It smells so good," John said.

Charlotte brought the pan around and dished them each up a good-sized portion of eggs and bacon. They thanked her and started eating right away. She laughed at them forgetting their manners. But manners didn't matter anymore, did they?

"What's the plan for today?" Aaron asked, looking at Charlotte. John also looked her way. She wasn't sure if they were faking their respect for her decisions or if they really did want her opinion. She felt weird having anyone look to her for directions. She was used to doing whatever she wanted, but that usually wasn't with the blessing of the men of the town.

"I need to go check on the tribe and see if Mica is around. When I went to get the tents for the others last week, her cousin Rem was still working at the store. So I don't think they went too far, yet."

The men nodded.

"We first need to check the paths again and make sure no one else is out there," John suggested. "Maybe Aaron can do another perimeter check today and we can start hauling some of the rations that the townsfolk left behind into the keepers' quarters to stockpile so we don't have to keep going into town to get what we need."

Charlotte agreed, "I think we should also make it a little harder for people to make it down the road to the lighthouse. It would be nice to control who is coming and going at least on the roadway."

"That sounds like a plan," Aaron said. "I will take one of Andrew's extra horses and head out after I finish eating."

When they finished their meal, Aaron packed a rifle and went out on one of the buckskin ponies. John and Charlotte started rummaging through the supply closet to take a survey of what they had and what they might need in the next few weeks.

"It seems like we have just about everything we need except we probably should try to find more supplies for any injuries and maybe even some extra wheat so we can add to the flour stock. We are getting a bit low after feeding all of the guests who stayed here recently," Charlotte told him.

He wrote it down and then told her they would need some additional feed for the horses if they were going to try to keep a few in the paddock for a while.

"Let's head into town and just hit up a few farms to see what they have," he suggested.

Charlotte agreed. Having more than what they need was certainly better than not having enough, especially with the weather being unpredictable in the summers and falls in that part of Florida. "I've noticed the winds picking up today," she said. "I think we better plan for a storm or two."

They grabbed her horse, Hershel and another mare from the herd and a few bags to pack the things they hoped to find along the way. Then they were off, heading towards the closest farm on the outskirts of town.

The Jamesons' place was a two-story bungalow with white, clapboard siding and a big, red barn. The structures were surrounded by tall grass fields that they had to carefully traverse so their horses wouldn't trip on anything hidden in the rushes. The townsfolk had left in the middle of one of the hay harvesting months and it was obvious that they had left a lot of hay to go to seed on the fields. This property was no exception.

Other things they had to watch out for were snakes. Florida snakes were nothing to shake a stick at, some of them could kill you with just one bite, especially without any doctors nearby with any ability to drain the wounds and suck out the poison. With abandoned ponds and wells, it was possible there could be moccasin snakes- the kind that don't like people or horses coming close to them at all and might even chase you in order to sink their super venomous fangs into something like a leg or a hoof. They certainly could not risk running into any snakes, or gators. But they didn't see any as they picked their way through the fields and made it to the front porch.

Charlotte ran inside to scope out the supplies in the house, while John made his way to the barn to see about borrowing a wagon and loading up some hay. Most of the barns had wagons, but Charlotte and Andrew's family rarely needed to haul much as lighthouse keepers, so they didn't have their own. Back when everyone was still in town, the Jamesons would have gladly loaned them the wagon or given them hay if they needed it, so they didn't feel bad taking what they needed. Besides, no one was planning to return anytime soon. The hay and food would go to waste anyway.

Soon, John returned to the house. "I found a bunch of hay and grain and loaded up the Jamesons' wagon and hitched up the horse. She seems to have some pulling experience," he laughed. "It would be a shame if she threw a fit and didn't take all that back for us!"

Charlotte laughed at the image of the horse running off with all the supplies he had loaded. But she knew most of the horses were trained for versatile activities out on the Florida frontier. Everyone used them for just about everything.

"I found a lot of things we can use, too. Can we put more on the wagon?" She motioned to the pile of items next to the door- bags of flour and spices and even some salted pork that could come in handy for dinners or lunches soon.

He nodded, then sauntered into the pantry area.

A few minutes later, as Charlotte finished taking some of the sacks to the wagon, John emerged again. He held a bottle against his damp shirt, laughing loudly. "Lookit what I found here!" he called to her across the room.

"Whatever it is, I don't think I want it if you're going to carry it with your sweaty shirt," she giggled.

"It smells like good ol' American whiskey," he laughed. "Or firewater, as your friends might call it."

Charlotte smiled and picked up another sack.

"Do you like whiskey, Charlotte," John's voice sounded much closer this time.

She turned and saw him holding a glass next to her face. She laughed, "I'm not particularly interested in whiskey, Mr. Thompson," she said. "I've always considered whiskey a man's drink. I prefer to keep my wits about me."

He sipped some of the whiskey from the bottle. "Oh, yes, this is definitely a man's drink, Charlotte DuBose. Definitely. But I will share it with you."

She shook her head. "I don't really need any," she insisted.

"Suit yourself," he laughed, and drank another swig from the bottle.

Just then, Charlotte noticed the snake. It had slithered into the room while they left the door open to haul out the supplies. It was black and red striped with some yellow.

Charlotte and John froze. "We need to get something to push him out of the entrance," John whispered. "We can't go anywhere with him there and I have a feeling he might get closer to us if we don't get him out quickly."

Charlotte thought fast and realized she had just what she needed. She took the bag of spices from the counter next to her and dropped it right next to the snake, between where they were standing and where the snake was heading their way. The loud noise next to it caused the snake to change direction and to retreat out into the grass. She grabbed the door and flung it shut, collapsing into the chair next to the kitchen table.

"That could have been really ugly," she said, fanning herself from the muggy air that seemed to be strangling her for a minute.

"It could have been," John agreed, wiping his own brow with his shirt. As he pulled the shirt up to reach his face, she glimpsed his perfectly rippled stomach for just a second. She looked away, embarrassed that he might have noticed.

"Well, Miss DuBose, I think you definitely deserve some whiskey now."

They both laughed, letting off some of the tension permeating the room.

"I agree, Mr. Thompson. I will go ahead and put my cautions to the side and take a little sip of your whiskey find."

He didn't waste any time getting the glass to her hand. She leaned back in the chair, slowly letting the thick fluid course down the back of her throat, savoring the way it burned as it went down.

"It's not bad," she said. "I might need to try a little more."

He laughed and filled her glass even higher.

She could feel herself relaxing and sinking into the chair more. "Do you think there are any other snakes inside this place?"

"Nah, I imagine that one just came in because we left the door wide open. But, we can check…" he stood up and walked towards the sitting room. "I don't see any in here…"

She stood up and followed him. The alcohol had clearly gone to her head already, as the room was spinning a little as she hobbled behind him. "Whoa!" she lost her balance a little and grabbed his arm that he reached out to steady her.

"I'm sorry," she laughed. "I don't usually indulge in whiskey enough to be able to handle much at all."

"We should probably have you sit down again," he said, leading her to the floral couch by the bay window.

She sat down abruptly, misjudging the distance of the cushion. They both giggled again, as she pulled him down next to her without intending to do so.

"I think I will sit with you then," he laughed, scooting over enough so they could both fit into the small seat. "Oh, this wasn't made for two adults, was it?"

She leaned into his shoulder, balancing her head against him for a minute, and laughed, "oh, I think we fit really well."

"Charlotte DuBose, I think you're drunk," John said, steadying her arm as she reached for the glass he had already taken from her. "You don't need anymore."

As her arm crossed in front of him, he froze. She was not drunk enough to miss the look on his face- something between longing and starvation.

She knew he was going to kiss her before he even leaned in. Perhaps it was her that was leaning in, she couldn't really tell. But somehow, they ended up wrapped up in each other's arms and his mouth was on hers. She could feel his warm breath on her own and taste the sweet whiskey on his tongue. She let him hold her and caress her as they kissed.

And then she pulled back and stared into his eyes. "John Thompson, what are you doing to me?"

He smiled, "I think what we've been wanting to do for quite a while, if I read the situation right."

She shook her head, "I can't do this," she said, while still leaning in for more kisses, more touches and caresses.

"You can't?" he whispered in between breaths. "It seems like you can. And you are."

She pulled away from his strong arms and fixed her dress around her. "I really can't, John. We have so many other things to worry about. I don't know how we can possibly focus on this sort of thing."

He grimaced, looking as if she had slapped him. Then he grabbed the sack of flour from the table and walked out the door.

She didn't know what to say at that point. She had to stop herself from racing out there after him. He hadn't done anything wrong. Her body was still pulled towards him like a magnet, and she felt her heart beating quickly in her chest.

Then she heard him calling to her and she ran to the doorway to see what was causing such an outburst when he was hellbent on not talking to her in the moment.

"Charlotte!" he yelled, "We need to go. We need to go now."

"What's wrong?" she asked, but she could see what he was talking about immediately. The wind had picked up and the few tree branches and palm fronds around the barn were battering against the sides of the structure.

"If we don't go now, we may get stuck here. You were right about the storm. Let's get these horses hitched and get out of here."

She ran to grab her horse and struggled next to John to strap the harnesses on the antsy animals. They soon were ready to ride and she hopped on the wagon bench beside him as he slapped the reins and the horses pranced forward in the wind.

"I hope Aaron is back at the light station already," John said, having to shout against the gusts that took his breath away from them.

She nodded. She couldn't bear to think of anything happening to Aaron. Especially when she was the one demanding they be able to talk with the tribe. He wouldn't be out there checking the route if she hadn't insisted.

She gripped the worn wood of the wagon side tightly and lowered her chin to her chest so she could breathe easier. This was more than a small storm- this was more like a tropical storm or even a hurricane. She could see the winds tearing the trees apart above them as they drove the horses into the clearing by the keepers' cottage. They quickly unhitched the horses and sent them into the large pasture where they could seek cover with the herd. Then they rushed to unload what they could from the wagon. The hay bales were already being torn apart from the wind as they threw them into the small barn. Then they grabbed as many sacks of supplies as they could hold and ran into the cottage. As they turned to go back and get the rest, they saw Aaron run from his cabin and grab the remaining items. He rushed into the cottage to meet them.

"You made it back," Charlotte couldn't help but grab his arm and pull him to her.

"I did, but it was close," he said, smiling down at her hug and then releasing her from his own grasp. "There was a small band of men camping down the road about two miles. I had a heck of a time trying to get around them to go towards the Mayaimi Seminoles' camp. Then, getting back here was even more difficult because the men had spread out more and were hunting in the trees. I almost ran into one really grisly man who saw the bushes move where I was standing. Luckily a deer ran through the clearing just then and took the attention off my position or I wouldn't be here right now."

"What do you mean? You really think they would have harmed you?" Charlotte gasped.

"Definitely," he said. "They were not there to make friends. They were clearly upset about the Indian War and were cussing and drinking heavily."

"Great," John Thompson said, shaking his head. "This is just what we need when things are already difficult. But maybe they will go north when they realize they are in the middle of a tropical storm."

The wind was tearing through the bushes behind the cottage with a whining noise that Charlotte had never heard during other tropical storms. They all stood quietly and watched as the world became crazier and crazier outside the windows.

"We should probably make sure the lens is safe in the tower," John brought them out of the trance.

Charlotte and Aaron both nodded and the three of them quickly rushed to the door and threw on their coats and boots before running to the tower stairs. The ground was saturated from the rain already and Charlotte could see the fencing damaged in several areas from the trees that had dropped limbs or fallen across the boards. She saw the white caps on the ocean just beyond the beach and had to grasp ahold of the doorway to be able to push her body inside. This was not a normal storm.

As they ran up the stairs and worked to cover the lens with additional blankets and put the extra storm boards around the windows of the light, Charlotte could only think of one thing. What would happen to the townsfolk and her brother's family in this kind of storm? Had they made it to Key West safely? She could only hope. This was one of those storms where you wouldn't want to be caught out in a boat. And what if it was worse somewhere else…?

She pushed those thoughts out of her head because she couldn't deal with those fears right now. They had to get the light safely secured and then get to safety themselves. The rain was pelting the windows behind the wood they installed, and the drafts were blowing inside so much that they could feel the spray of rain even from in the room. It was going to be a rough one. She hoped the old lens would hold up. It withstood many storms in the past, but if they lost even one of the panels of handcrafted glass prisms it would be a horrible hassle to try to replace the parts. Getting a new first order Fresnel lens during the wars and with all of the increased travel scrutiny would be near impossible. This lens was only about a decade old anyway and the new technology that created this amazing way to direct light for such long distances was not inexpensive.

She looked at John and Aaron who were tying the last ropes to secure the lens in the little room. Then they motioned her to go downstairs with them. The storm was so loud that they could no longer communicate by voice.

Once they were outside and bolted the door to the frame with the large security bar, they rushed back across the yard. This time they had to hold onto each other and practically crawl against the wind that was blowing off the ocean. The waves were crashing against the shore and breaking around their feet. The idea of sandbagging the property was futile at this point. They didn't have enough people and they didn't have enough notice. Charlotte remembered past storms coming slowly enough across the water from Cuba that they had some indication of the severity so they could sandbag all around and keep the water from flooding the buildings. But they would have to take their chances this time. Without people manning the telegraph station in town or helping with weather forecasts, they were at the mercy of nature and without notice this time.

They reached the door of the cottage and it swung open so hard that it broke one of the hinges at the top of the door. John and Aaron struggled with it and were able to shut it. "We'll fix that hinge later," Aaron called to her. She nodded. That wasn't important now. But making sure it stayed closed was definitely a priority. They moved the large dresser from the hallway against the doorway to block the additional wind and rain that was curling around the gaps in the door frame already. If the door opened, at least there would be one more barrier to the storm before the rain caused even more damage.

"Let's go in the brick storage room" John pointed, and they rushed towards it.

"Wait," Charlotte called as they raced towards the back room. "I want to grab some blankets and other things just in case we need them."

"There's not enough time," Aaron said, running back to grab her arm and pull her to the doorway. She relented and they almost tumbled into the darkness together. John caught her other arm as she stumbled into the room. He led her to the back corner where he turned some wooden boxes on their sides. This was where they would be stuck until the winds let up.

Hopefully the rain that was pouring down would not flood the building, or at least not the room they were barricading themselves inside. She knew the house was built on a foundation that gave them some leeway between the sands of the beach and the floor. But it would be close if the rain continued to fall as hard as it was falling when they were outside.

John found an extra lantern and some matches and lit up the room. They could hear the building groaning around them, with what Charlotte imagined could be the sounds of cracking mortar and bricks. She wondered how the wooden porches would hold up and hoped the ocean wouldn't take the whole building away with them in it. They sat silently. No one wanted to chit chat and there was really nothing they could do but pray and hope they would weather this storm okay. They had work to do and if the light itself was affected, they would be unable to do much at all. She wasn't sure what the Lighthouse Service would do if they were out of commission. They may close down the entire site and make them go down to Key West too. Her mind raced, thinking about the "what ifs" and wondering about her brother's safety and that of his family and the other towns people.

Chapter Nine

It seemed like the storm went on for days. When it finally calmed enough for them to open the door and peek out, Charlotte realized it was nightfall already.

They ventured into the living area of the home. The furniture and knickknack decorations were cockeyed across the floor, and the couches and chairs were soaking wet. She noticed a few broken windows and several inches of water on the floor near the entryway. But the building seemed to have withstood the storm okay, structurally.

"I'm going to check on the light," John called to them, and Aaron agreed to go along. Charlotte didn't wait for their permission to follow them too. It took a while to get the door open. A huge palm tree had wedged itself against the frame and it would not budge. Aaron was able to get out the back door and run around the house to move the tree away and off the porch. There were broken boards all over, but they were able to carefully make their way to the sand below. There were new tide pools around the house, but the water had gone down enough that it seemed safe to cross the yard to the light tower.

At least the tower was still standing. It was full of about three feet of water inside though. A lot rushed out and around their boots when they pried the door open. They slogged through it and up the stairway. Luckily the boards had kept the windows from breaking. Everything seemed okay and they were able to get the wick dry enough to light the flame after pouring some additional kerosene in the tank.

"I think she should be good to go tonight," John sighed.

Charlotte leaned against the railing next to the window. "I was so worried about the lens. I couldn't bear to imagine if anything had happened to it."

Aaron smiled across the darkening room and she held his gaze. John noticed their connection and shuffled towards the other side of the lens. Charlotte hadn't even had time to think about what happened at the Jamesons' farmhouse. And she certainly didn't want to get wrapped up in any emotional drama. She ignored John's reaction and she helped Aaron move some of the boards down the staircase to store them below.

"I sure hope there won't be any more wind tonight," she said.

"It seems really calm out there now," Aaron pointed out the open doorway to the gentle lapping of the waves against the big rocks that protected the lighthouse. Much different than when the waves were way above those rocks and pounding against the stucco siding of the light tower.

She nodded. She was exhausted and happy that the men agreed that they would finish cleaning things up tomorrow. Right now, they all needed some sleep. She found them all some dry blankets and everyone agreed that it was better if the men stayed with Charlotte on the second floor. They bedded down in the spare bedroom that used to be used for Andrew's kids. Charlotte was happy to see her bedroom ceilings and even the roof had withstood all the winds okay and her bed was dry. She fell into the covers and didn't wake up until daybreak.

In the morning when she went to turn off the light and cover the windows so the lens wouldn't start any fires from the sun shining on it, she found the men outside, checking out the damage in the daylight. It looked much worse than she imagined. The bushes were all torn apart, and the land looked like someone had hacked up all of the greenery into stalks of dead branches. The sand by the water was moved all around and there were large gashes of new waterways where the water never used to be. There was debris everywhere. She saw that the barn siding was down in parts but luckily it seemed as if most of the hay stayed dry in the center of the building.

The old outhouse was crooked. The men worked on stabilizing it so Charlotte could use it.

"It would be a shame if the lady didn't have anywhere to relieve herself," they laughed. Finding humor in the grim reality helped a little. Charlotte tried to focus on what needed to be done now. But she was overwhelmed by the mess.

"I am going to need to ride into town and see if I can get on the telegraph at the news office. I want to hear how Key West held up against those winds," John said as they finished moving some of the biggest debris from the front porch area.

Charlotte sighed. She was so nervous about her brother's family that she could barely think about it without wincing. She hoped they had found somewhere safe to stay and were settled down there by now.

Aaron helped John work on resetting the lighthouse door and then the two of them fixed the hinge on the house. Then they went out to the pasture to see if they could find the horses. Charlotte took the quiet time to rearrange the furniture and start mopping some of the water off the wood floors. Much of it had drained through some of the cracks between the boards in the corners. She wanted to make sure it was nice and dry so it would be less likely to mold later.

By the time she was done, Aaron returned.

"I'm happy to say that the horses all seem to be out there. I also saw some of the pigs and chickens. It's amazing how resilient animals can be in a huge storm."

Charlotte smiled. She had worried about Hershel and was happy to hear they would have enough of the other animals to continue to have meat and eggs available if they ran out of the salted stuff in the pantry.

"Do you think that was just a tropical storm?" she asked. "It seemed really strong."

He shrugged. "I'm not sure. But it definitely was a huge storm. One of the biggest I've ever seen."

She nodded. "I sure hope we have good news from Key West."

"Yeah, me too."

They finished moving some of the larger items in the room back to where they went and then Aaron headed back outside to work on clearing the lot. Charlotte started to plan out the day's meals.

When John rode back into the property and unsaddled, he sauntered inside the house and tossed his boots in the corner.

"Well," he said, "there's news that Key West was hit pretty hard from that storm last night."

Charlotte and Aaron rushed over to hear more.

"It sounds like much of the rail lines were destroyed and a lot of the workers who were working on the new road who live in the shacks along the route in Marathon were hurt pretty badly. It sounds like most were killed."

"Oh no," Charlotte gasped. "What about our families and friends? What about Andrew and his family?"

"I don't know anything specific yet. Hopefully more news will come over the telegraph soon." They all hung their heads.

"At this point we just need to keep doing what we stayed here to do- keeping that light running and watching out for intruders," Aaron said.

"What happened to that group of men that Aaron saw the other day?" Charlotte asked. "Did you see them?"

"No, I didn't see any sign of anyone. I didn't go very far though- maybe they holed up in one of the abandoned houses further in town," John said.

"I hope they got nice and scared and go away," Charlotte replied. They certainly didn't need any hotheaded renegades trying to mess with their light station. At least they were coming by land so they wouldn't see the light as much as if they were coming by sea. If they weren't aware of the light station, they may avoid it altogether.

"We still need to check on Mica's family," Charlotte reminded them. "I wonder how they did with the storm. They don't have a lot of solid housing at their camp."

Since Mica's family were aware of the policies of the United States government in Florida, they were living a much more transient life. Their farming ways were changed to mostly travel with cattle now. But they had settled in that Key Biscayne region for a long time so far. Charlotte hoped they wouldn't have to move anytime soon, but she heard the rumors about the troops circling the area and trying to attack the villages to make the Natives move onto reservations. They had a reservation just to the north in the Lake Okeechobee region and Mica had expressed anxiety about her family being forced to live there in the future.

"We are the last of the Mayaimi tribes that haven't been killed or moved to reservations," Mica told her months ago. "If they make us move, it would kill so many of us to have to give up our freedoms. But there are some Creek tribes that have come down here and joined the Seminoles who are willing to fight. At some point it could get really awful," Mica warned her. "You might not want to come to our camps when we get to that kind of situation. It wouldn't be safe for you."

But Charlotte was devastated to think of the peaceful friends she knew having to move or to hide.

"It's important that we get to their camp soon. What if they need help?" She asked Aaron and John.

"Let's give it a couple of days so they can regroup from the storm and so we can wait and see what those men Aaron saw are up to. I don't want to be in such a hurry that we get blindsided by those awful people and everyone, including us and the tribe folks, are at a disadvantage."

Charlotte wasn't sure she could wait days. It was scary to think of what could happen if the tribe wasn't safe. Especially if those men were creeping around. The stories she heard about how rogue soldiers were torturing Natives made her cringe. It wasn't worth waiting long. If Aaron and John were not in a hurry, she might need to do it on her own.

She knew the forest well and had traversed the paths through the thickest parts of the palm jungle her whole life with Mica and Rem and the other kids. She wasn't afraid of the venomous snakes or gators or other things she figured the other white men would be scared of. She could make it by the back trails and at least check on things and be back before lunch. She decided she would have to do it. If only for her peace of mind.

"I am going to check on Hershel," she said, pointing to where the herd was grazing way across the back pasture under the trees. The men were in the middle of working on one of the fences and they just nodded in acknowledgement.

She quietly walked over to the barn and grabbed his halter and a bareback pad. Then she had to keep herself from running across the grass, so they didn't notice her streaking across the property with those items and wonder what she was up to. She found Hershel and readied him for their journey. Then she quickly opened the front gate and slipped through to the left of the road where a discrete path began.

She took this route often, but it was torn up from the windstorm and she had to get off Hershel and walk him around several fallen trees. Some areas were really mucky from water intrusion, and she hoped she wouldn't get stuck where she couldn't cross. Luckily, she continued to find her way around the debris and mud and back to the trail, over and over.

She kept her eyes peeled for any signs of trouble. But it was a quiet ride for the most part, aside from bird calls and the loud crickets who were singing out warnings to their friends as she led Hershel through some tall grass areas.

Chapter Ten

As she rounded the last bend in the trail, she could hear a commotion at the Mayaimi tribe's camp area. A man's voice was yelling loudly in English but she wasn't close enough to understand what he was saying.

She got off Hershel and walked him slowly towards the back of the wooden barn that the tribe used to store their supplies. The camp was mostly tents and temporary structures made of wood and reeds; a blend between the white culture and the Natives' traditional housing. The barn had been a joint effort that the townsfolk donated to the tribe as part of one of their trade deals many years ago. It provided a good place for Charlotte to get close enough to see what was going on.

She noticed that most of the other structures were tattered and torn, likely from the recent storm. She didn't see a lot of tribe members. Actually, the camp seemed pretty deserted.

But right in the middle of the path between the barn and the first set of tents she could see a group of about five or six really dirty and scruffy white men. They were standing around in what appeared to be a circle. And to her dismay, she could see Mica's cousin, Rem stuck with his arms behind his body, between the arms of one of the bigger men.

She knew Rem needed help, and quick. Gathering up her skirt, she ran into the clearing screaming at the top of her lungs- "don't you dare touch this boy," she yelled. "He hasn't done one thing to you and if you harm him, I will be the witness to the military tribunal who will surely capture you and make you hang for harming a child."

The men, who at first seemed surprised at her entrance, now looked at each other and laughed. "Oh? And you believe you will have that chance?" The one with the longest and dirtiest beard chuckled. "It looks like we now have twice the fun ahead."

Rem's eyes were large as he stared at the big shotgun the short and quieter man held against his chest.

Charlotte sneered right back at the men and scuffed her feet as she slid towards them, refusing to show any fear. If they sensed that they had the upper hand, then Charlotte and Rem both were doomed. The only thing she could come up with was thinking of them as schoolyard bullies, and without fear they didn't have much. Except guns... but this might buy her a little more time.

"You need to let him go immediately and you need to get off our island," she yelled back towards the men, and she grabbed for Hershel's reins next to her.

The bearded guy reached the horse first and yanked him away from her reach, then he grabbed her arm and twisted her into a position under his arm like they were holding Rem. "I don't think you understand," he said. "You ain't going anywhere, except where we say."

Charlotte coughed from the weight of his arm across her neck. She couldn't move much, but she could almost reach the knife in his belt on his other hip. If he would only move her a little more towards that side, she might be able to grab it.

She watched as the little guy forced Rem to put his hands out. Then he wrapped the other set of horse reins around them and jerked Rem to follow as they led the horses deeper into the woods and Charlotte was forced to stumble along with the quick gait of the man who had her pinned against his armpit, which was really starting to penetrate her nose with sweat-soaked flesh that likely hadn't been washed in days.

It seemed like they trudged through acres and acres, when finally, they came to an abrupt halt. She looked up and caught a quick glimpse of a flash of metal, heard some gun shots, and then she was thrown down away from the men and yanked into some thick palm bushes.

When she finally got her sense of direction back and her eyes could focus, she realized she was being held again, but this time by softer hands that covered her mouth.

The men shot their guns towards something with haphazard aim, as they were also jerked down to the ground. But Charlotte could tell the hands that held them were not as gentle as the ones securing her. A group of young Seminole men had pinned her and Rem down.

The rest of the bodies popped out of the bushes along the trail and squirmed as they quickly tied the horrid white men up with leather rope, and then tied them to their horses the same way Rem had been tied before they had released him.

Then the Natives yelled and smacked the horses and the white men were dragged through the bushes, screaming at first and then going silent as they conked against pine trees and palms and their bodies thunked across the ground. Eventually, Charlotte could tell from the silence that they stopped when they made it pretty far into the distance. Perhaps the horses had reached the main road, and were waiting for further direction, like they were trained to do.

Charlotte turned around and looked up to see Mica's serious face staring down at her. She could have passed out from the relief that flooded her whole body. "Mica!" She whispered, "I was so worried about you."

Mica motioned her to stay quiet. She did not seem as happy to see Charlotte as Charlotte was to see her. They both glanced at where Rem stood with the other Natives. They had him untied and he was rubbing his chafed and bruised hands and talking quickly in their language so fast that Charlotte couldn't follow.

They motioned to where Mica held Charlotte and moved towards her with heavy steps.

She saw Rem grab their arms and hold them back, while Mica walked towards them to join in the conversation.

Charlotte stayed where Mica left her, worried that she would also become a target of their anger as a white person. But eventually the men looked her direction and motioned again to Mica and Rem and walked away. Charlotte imagined that they were likely telling Mica to get Charlotte out of there.

"You should not have come here," Mica said when she returned to Charlotte's side. "It's much too dangerous. There are more of those soldiers. This was just one group. More will come. And we have to leave."

Charlotte hung her head. "I'm sorry, Mica. I didn't mean to cause any trouble. But they were hurting Rem and I wasn't sure where the rest of you were. I saw your camp. How did you survive that awful storm?"

Mica shrugged. "We are strong. Don't ever doubt that we will make it. But by coming here you have made it more dangerous for us. More of your people will follow you here."

"Well," Charlotte said, "our town is empty now. I didn't want those men to know, but everyone left to go to Key West."

Mica's eyes widened. "We wondered why we had not heard from anyone from your town in a few days."

"Yeah," Charlotte continued, "they left because they heard about the wars between the Seminole and the U.S. government. People are dying on both sides and there were some recent massacres of white people across the bay. I knew it wasn't your tribe. But others thought that we were at risk."

Mica scoffed, "that THEY were at risk? Hmph. It is obvious that we are the ones who are being rounded up and killed by the white people. It's good they left. I'm sorry, I care about you. But we are being killed and you are not welcome here anymore."

Those words, although expected and deserved, hit Charlotte right in the heart. "I understand," she whispered. "I'm sorry."

Mica shrugged. "It isn't like before. We can't be friends, Charlotte. You have to leave, and you have to find your people in Key West and stay down there. There are more white men coming to harm us. And there are some very angry groups of Mayaimi and Creek warriors who are not going to know or care about our friendship. You are in danger. We are both in danger."

Charlotte nodded. She knew this was the likely discussion they would have. But it hurt all the same. "I will miss you, Mica," she whispered back. "You are my friend and I will find you again."

Mica nodded, "perhaps."

She pushed Charlotte's arm so that she was facing the path back to the camp and that would lead her back to her light station beyond.

One of the other young Mayaimi boys walked towards her, leading Hershel. He motioned to her to take the reins. She had no idea how her horse was still there, but she knew the Mayaimi were skilled horse people and likely were able to round him up when they chased those men away.

"We are leaving, Charlotte. And you should do the same. Go find your brother and your friends. Be safe." Mica walked with her to the edge of the thicket. Then she turned and surprised Charlotte by touching her arm. "I hope the spirits bless you, Charlotte."

Charlotte felt her tears start to slide out of her eyes. "I will miss you, Mica." Then she jumped up on Hershel's back and took one last look behind her.

Mica walked back to the others and they headed back into the grass and palm fronds. Charlotte wondered if she would ever see them again. So many memories of the good years played inside her mind. At least they are safe, she told herself. At least they weathered that storm. But she knew there were likely to be more storms of various types headed their way.

She got Hershel into a trot and rushed back towards the light station. Now she needed to find out what happened with Andrew and the rest of the townspeople. If they didn't make it through the storm, she didn't know what she would do.

Chapter Eleven

Charlotte barely made it to the end of the path when she heard John and Aaron yelling her name. They were scouring the edge of the road and looking for horse tracks. Aaron just discovered the way the hoof prints led to the path Charlotte took, when Charlotte came around the bend and he saw her riding towards him.

"John," Aaron called behind him, "I found her!"

"Oh, thank God," John yelled back to Aaron and then ran towards the path. "Charlotte, where the hell were you?"

"I'm sorry I worried you," Charlotte began.

But John cut her off, "Charlotte you're bleeding all over your dress. We need to get you in the house." He grabbed Hershel's reins and then grabbed Charlotte around the waist and slid her off the horse and into his arms.

She started shaking. Until she felt the security of his grasp, she had been managing to convince herself that she was fine. But she really was not fine and could feel her body react to the shock of the last hour.

"Those men…" she started but couldn't finish.

"Mica… Rem…" she gasped. It was all too much. She let herself be carried across the road and down the driveway to the house, where Aaron opened the door so John could carry her inside and up the stairs to her bed. He laid her down on the sheets and helped her unlace her shoes.

"I don't know what happened, but it sounds awful. And you're hurt," John said softly. He moved her hair from across her cheek and put his hand gently against the side of her face. "I'm so glad you're back."

She mustered a little smile. It felt good to hear him say he was worried about her. She let him help her sit up and help her take off the topcoat of her dress. She knew it wasn't appropriate to have a man help her undress, but she was sore from being jerked around by the renegade men and then tackled by the Natives. She hadn't realized how many cuts and bruises she ended up with all over her arms and legs. She had a small gash in the side of her shoulder that was bleeding through her clothing.

Aaron came up the stairs with a bowl of warmed water and a wet rag. John took the rag from him and washed Charlotte's injuries, slowing as she winced whenever the water touched her skin.

Aaron looked a little put out by John taking over but he shrugged and walked out of the room. She could hear him go back down the stairs. He called back to them to let them know he was going to take care of the horses and would be right back. Charlotte was surprised at how exhausted she felt. And achy.

After cleaning her wounds, John carefully applied some bandages on the one on her shoulder. "That was a pretty deep cut, Charlotte," he told her.

"I will be okay," she smiled.

John leaned towards her again and this time he surprised her by kissing the top of her head as he finished checking another wound. "I was so worried," he said, and then in the same soft voice warned her, "don't ever do such a stupid thing again."

"I know…But I went because I needed to check on Mica," she protested. But she could see his stern face. "Okay, I know I should have waited for you."

He sat next to her on the bed, reaching to help pull her dress back up and over her bandages. She let him move her like she was a doll. When he sat back against the headboard she naturally leaned back into his arms. It went against her insistence of staying out of emotional drama, but she wanted to feel him next to her so badly.

He turned her head and torso around so she could look towards him, and he stared into her eyes. "Charlotte DuBose you are stubborn and ridiculous and dangerous. But I still can't help but want to kiss you."

She felt him hard against her as he pulled her closer. She felt the ragged section of his shirt under her chin where he'd ripped the shoulder and a patch was sewn in it that stood out from the rest of the shirt.

Her body melted into his as her lips met his mouth and she felt him all around her.

And then he pulled away just as suddenly.

She couldn't help but gasp for air after such an abrupt departure.

"Aaron will be back soon," he said, pretending like nothing had just happened.

He helped her scoot over to where she was balanced on the pillows instead of his chest. "You should rest for a bit," he told her. "I have to go get some more things done."

He stood up and walked out the door without her being able to read any expression on his face.

She wasn't sure what made him leave so suddenly. But after she stopped breathing so heavy and got a hold of her raging emotions, she realized she was actually somewhat relieved that he had left before things got even more heated.

She couldn't think very long. She noticed the room blurring a bit. Then she fell asleep and dreamed about playing at the beach with her Mayaimi friends.

She woke around midnight and realized she had slept all day. Aaron was asleep on the chair next to her bed. He didn't look very comfortable with his knees curled up around him on the sides of the hard chair and his chin against his chest. She was surprised he was there, especially at that time of night.

When she stirred even just slightly, he jumped to an alert pose. "Are you okay, Charlotte?" he whispered.

She nodded slowly then started to ramble, "I must have missed lunch and dinner. I'm sorry you had to sit here and wait for me. You don't look really comfortable. And did you eat?"

His chuckle surprised her. "Slow down," he laughed, "Of course, we ate. And why are you worrying about us after what you went through?"

She moved her sore shoulder and felt a sharp stabbing pain. "Ugh… Why am I hurting worse now? I wasn't hurting this badly before."

"You had quite a deep cut on that shoulder, and I imagine you bruised it pretty badly too."

He leaned over and moved the neck of her dress so he could check on her bandages. "Leave those on there for a couple days. I think they will heal okay. John bandaged them up well."

Charlotte nodded. "Any news about Key West yet?"

Aaron shook his head and his mouth tensed. "I think we will have to check the telegraph again soon. Maybe there's more news."

She nodded. That would be a good plan, but she knew it was too late now to do it that night.

"Hey, Charlotte," Aaron said even more quietly. "I need to ask you something."

"What, Aaron? Ask me anything."

"I think John stayed behind with you because he is interested in pursuing more of a relationship with you." He squirmed a little, seeming uncomfortable going down this path of questioning. "Are you okay with that?"

"What makes you think that?" she whispered back, feigning awe.

"He seems really interested in making sure you are okay. I mean, don't get me wrong, that isn't a bad thing."

She smiled. "You seem that way too."

He looked away a little, then said, "Charlotte, I love you like a sister. I do. I will do anything to make sure you're okay. We've been very close friends for years. And you are beautiful…" he hesitated. "But it's not something either of us would ever push further. We just couldn't."

"Thank you, Aaron. That means a lot to me. We never talk about that aspect of our friendship."

"I think we are in two different worlds, but I think your heart is in the right place. And you're a pain in the ass, which makes me laugh. I think you're pretty great."

They both laughed.

He reached for her hand and held it, her chalk white skin even brighter against his deep brown hand. She liked the way it felt to have him hold her hand. An element of comfort and familiarity because he had been her best friend for years. But also, she liked knowing she could do it and no one would be able to stop her. She spent her whole life being told how she should act with people with darker skin than hers. But it never made sense to her. She adored Aaron. Yet, if Andrew was around, she would be yelled at, and Aaron never would have even dared such a move if he was there. She was disappointed in herself for thinking about those things. No one was there to judge them. It was not improper if they were in their own world, right?

John was in the other room. John, whose touch made her warm in all sorts of places that scared and amazed her. But Aaron was more than that, and she wanted his opinion and to make sure he wasn't hoping for something more with her before she would ever feel okay moving onto loving anyone else.

"We both know I need to get out of here, Charlotte," Aaron said, staring directly at her with his big brown eyes. "I am going to head over to the Bahamas soon. I want to be with the rest of my family who moved there when I was younger."

Charlotte knew Aaron used to talk about his family in the Bahamas. "That would be great, Aaron. I think you should do that."

"About ten years ago, before the lighthouse was built here, this used to be one of the points where Black people were able to load boats that took them to safety and freedom in the Bahamas," he told her. "Did you know that?"

She nodded, "Mica told me about it years ago. I didn't know if it was a true story or one of the stories she told me that she made up. But it makes sense."

Aaron nodded. "Well, now that we have a chance to rebuild our lives and no one is here to stop us, I think we both need to move towards things that we want to do."

Charlotte squeezed his hand. "I agree, Aaron. I think we do need to do that." She looked down at their hands. "I love you, sweet friend. I want you to be happy and free. I can't imagine what could happen if the troops show up here."

"Well, from what I hear, they are capturing Black people and trying to find where they potentially escaped from. If they catch me, I don't even think the papers we drew up with Andrew will help me now. Especially because he is gone to Key West."

She nodded. He was right. No matter how selfishly she wanted him to stay with her, or how much she adored him, she needed him to be safe and he deserved her support. He had always helped her and her family and still was doing so, even though he could have left already.

"When will you go?" she asked.

"I'm not sure. I can't wait much longer or the chances of the troops coming here to check on things will increase every day. I think I will wait a couple more weeks. Maybe longer. I want to make sure Andrew comes back for you first."

"I think I will be okay here with John," Charlotte surprised herself by saying. Deep down, she knew she was likely very safe with John. But the things he made her feel made her nervous.

"I think he would take good care of you," Aaron said.

"Wait, I think I would be fine with him here. But that's different than needing anyone to take care of me!" she laughed.

He chuckled. "But, Charlotte, I worry about those bands of Natives who are angry about the white policies. They won't care if you're a friend of Mica's. They won't differentiate between you and any other white person. But the tribes have been accepting Black people in, to join in the fight against the troops. So, with me here, you have a little more chance at being safe."

She shook her head. "I don't think they will be as friendly as you think they will. You're here helping white people without running off. If you want to be safe, you should go soon. If they find you here trying to help us, you're much more at risk."

"I'm not leaving you, Charlotte. Not yet," he said.

"Well, you should at least sleep on a real bed," she smiled. "Do you want to just sleep up here with me? There are no rules anymore, remember?"

He laughed. "No, my dear. I cannot do that. I might get myself into some trouble with that oaf in the other room if I were to try such a thing. He seems harmless and kind most of the time. But I imagine if I started sleeping in the same bed as you, he might protest just a bit."

They both laughed.

"What will I do with him?" Charlotte asked, half joking, but also curious what Aaron thought of the situation.

"I think you don't worry about all that kind of stuff until you know you aren't going to be captured by Indians or sent to the brig for harboring an escaped slave," he smiled to soften his words.

"I think you're right. I am trying to stay out of any drama. I can't handle any relationship messes while trying to keep the light lit. Besides, Andrew will be back soon and then we will probably need to turn the light over to the troops anyway. I'll have plenty of time later to worry about romance."

He nodded. "Let's just get you healed up and keep you from running into more trouble with all the people who want to kill you, okay?"

She grinned. "Okay."

"And get some sleep."

"I will," she promised. She was pleasantly surprised to have him lean over and give her a giant hug. His arms felt wonderful around her. And although she enjoyed his nearness and the comfort of him there, she was glad to realize there was no special spark there like she felt when John held her. That helped her with the conflicts in her head at least. Her loyalty to Aaron was not going to get in the way of whatever she was going to do with John. That was quite a relief. She sighed and let him go. She really was tired.

She watched him wrap up in the blanket he had around his shoulders and stumble sleepily into the other room where she could hear John's deep breathing.

She smiled. Everything would be okay. She was home safe and tomorrow she would hopefully get word that Andrew and his family were okay after the hurricane. Mica and Rem and their families were on their way to safer places. And Aaron was okay with John's interest in her.

For now, all of that was enough. She closed her eyes and was soon back asleep and dreaming.

Chapter Twelve

John had some bad news for them in the morning. He went back to the telegraph office and was able to contact the news people in Key West.

The report said that the storm was actually a hurricane- with some of the strongest winds ever to make landfall. Islamorada, about halfway down the Keys, took a direct hit. There were a lot of casualties. They predicted hundreds dead.

Charlotte cried at the news when John relayed it to them at the house. "And our friends? My family?" she asked.

John shook his head. "I don't have any names right now and the communication network is spotty."

"But they must have reached Key West by then," Aaron said. "Let's have hope that they were down there and housed in actual buildings. The storm hit Islamorada worst. Key West is about the same distance from

Islamorada as we are from Islamorada. It's possible they had heavy winds and lots of rain like we did, but they could have survived." He turned to John, "there are survivors, right?"

John nodded. "There are many more than a few hundred people in the Keys. And the reports I received are more about Islamorada than anywhere else. Let's keep hope that they made it and they are okay. We need to await news from your brother when he is able to send information."

But the reports did not get any better the rest of the week. Each day, John went to the telegraph office and returned with a new tidbit.

"The storm surge was twenty feet high at Islamorada," he said on Wednesday, bowing his head in sorrow.

"But the Keys are only a few feet above sea level," Charlotte gasped.

"People who tied themselves to the trees survived, I heard," John said. "If they were in buildings, they could have made it. They would have gotten wet, I'm sure. But they wouldn't wash away…"

On Thursday, he had to tell them, "it went straight down the Keys. Key West also took a pretty direct hit."

Charlotte gasped yet again. "My poor brother and Catharine and the kids…"

On Friday they received a copy of the Fort Lauderdale newspaper story. "408 people dead," it said, "People caught in the open were blasted by sand with such force that it stripped away their clothing." "259 of the dead were World War I veterans living in three Civilian Conservation Corps camps while they worked on building the Overseas Highway."

There were also reports of the train company not sending trains to rescue the people off the highway project. And one of the trains swept off the tracks in the storm surge.

It was so awful. Charlotte could hardly bear to hear the news. But she craved every piece of information she could gather because she wanted to know about her family and friends. Unfortunately, the news was never about Key West. Which could be a good thing, or a bad thing. What happened in Key West? What happened to Andrew and Catharine and the kids?

She was beside herself with worry.

John tried to lighten the mood, telling her that statistically not many other people died after accounting for the CCC workers. But that didn't feel like good news. Those poor men and women in Islamorada. Those poor families.

She waited each day for John to return from the telegraph office, often pacing by the door or standing in the yard watching the livestock in the fields. She tried to stay busy with light station chores, but her mind always went directly to thinking about the hurricane and aftermath.

Would Andrew be able to return to get them? With Flagler's train tracks supposedly damaged beyond easy repair and the road project completely gutted, his only option would be by boat. Was his boat safe from the hurricane winds? Would he have any way to get back there? She knew that in the best-case scenario, he would be much later than he promised originally. And what if he was hurt or dead or even missing? She could barely stand to think those "what ifs." And yet, that's all she could think about.

And the news continued to be awful.

Charlotte kept the lighthouse running smoothly in the hopes that the light would be a beacon for her brother if he dared to come by sea. It would be easier to cross the Intercoastal Waterway like the way they left, weeks ago. But with the increased Native presence and men like those awful ones that tried to kidnap her and Rem, still hanging around, she hoped he would find a safe way to come home. The Atlantic Ocean was a decent way to come if he was in a big enough ship. But she wasn't sure what he would have access to.

She hoped the military would help him. Maybe if he told them about his position as the lighthouse keeper and that they were still there manning the light, they would help him reach the island. She could only hope…

John was worried about Charlotte feeling so anxious and sad. He made every effort to help with the chores around the station. He hauled the kerosene up to the lamp and woke early each day to help her close the window shades. He and Aaron both made sure that the livestock were fed. At one point they had to chance running back with the wagon to the Jamesons' farm to get more feed for the extra animals they'd taken on when the townsfolk abandoned so many.

On one of their journeys to town, they returned with a surprise for her. She didn't know what to expect when they called her outside. "We have something for you. Maybe it will keep you from being so depressed," John said. Aaron stood by the wagon, smiling and holding something below the sides of the vehicle.

"What is it?" she asked, curiosity getting the best of her, even though she was trying to act stern about them bringing anything extra for her.

Aaron stood back away from the wagon and a little, furry head popped up. She took a second look and could see it was a puppy head.

"Awww!" she ran over to the wagon and looked in. A baby German Shepherd stared back at her, jumping up and down and wiggling its tail, half excited and likely half-terrified.

"Where did this little one come from?" she asked.

"We found it wandering around one of the barns at the Lewis farm when we stopped by there to check on their feed supply," Aaron stated. "Their dog must have had puppies at some point right before they left. We looked and couldn't find any trace of other dogs, so this one somehow must have been left behind, or it was the only one that survived being left there."

Charlotte reached out and the puppy retreated for a minute, then curiously approached her hand and gave it a big lick. "Is it a boy or girl?" she asked.

John took at handful of the puppy's scruff around its neck and picked the wiggly dog up and looked. "This one is definitely a girl," he laughed.

The dog seemed a bit put out about being manhandled, but soon came back around, begging for scratches on its head.

"I'm surprised she is so friendly after being left feral," Charlotte said.

"We were too," said Aaron. "I was not sure we should try to catch her, but she came right to us when we opened up a container of beans. She was so hungry."

"She looks pretty well-fed," Charlotte said.

"She probably had a mom around for a while. But we couldn't find any sign of her," John explained.

"Well, that's sad. I'm so glad you brought this one home," Charlotte said.

"What do you want to call her?" John asked.

"Hmmm," she thought for a minute. "I'm so obsessed about the horrible things that happened with the hurricane. But this little puppy is a positive thing to think about after such a scary event. I think I want to call her Stormy."

The men nodded. "Sounds good. Stormy it is," John agreed.

So, then the days seemed much brighter for Charlotte. She had something new and cuddly and fun to think about with Stormy running around the property. Andrew never wanted domestic animals except the livestock they used for food purposes. He said they made messes and he had to take care of the light station so he couldn't risk the hassle.

But Andrew wasn't there, and Charlotte didn't know if or when he would return. She just made sure to keep things clean and Stormy seemed to catch on quickly to the training. The days were going by quicker with Stormy to play with too.

Charlotte noticed that John watched her when she was laughing and playing with Stormy. Her eyes caught glimpses of him grinning in a way she hadn't seen him grin in a long time. Like her, he worried about the people who went to Key West. There still was no word about how Key West faired.

Except there was a story that they received from the Key West Inquirer, the new newspaper down there. It was about a damaged lightship- the Lightship Florida, which was stationed at Carysfort, an island off the coast of the Key Largo area. It wasn't about Key West exactly, which was many miles away. But the fact that the Inquirer was publishing at all was a good sign. They were hopeful that someone would send more news soon. They continued to check every day, but most days were just disappointing.

Charlotte took pride in polishing the brass in the lighthouse tower until it shined brightly, and she was meticulous in getting all the wicks ready each night and keeping the windows clean and clear in the evenings and then covered each morning. Shine on, shine off. She kept things operating as if the Lighthouse Service was coming to visit every day. And sometimes she wondered if they ever would visit again. With all the Indian War troubles, she figured they were staying clear of Florida. They had enough other lights to check on.

The days continued to go by, one after another. And still no Andrew.

Chapter Thirteen

John got an idea that they should build a better fence around the light station. There was a lot of hurricane debris around the local farms that he could see as he went back and forth to town to check the telegraph messages. He figured no one would mind if they gathered some of the wood and metal sheets that had piled up in the fields. It would be near impossible to figure out who to return them to, and besides, they had no idea when the property owners would return anyway.

"I think if we head into the town area, we are sure to get enough things to make a much stronger fence. It won't keep Indians out, but it will definitely slow them down if they have to try to cut metal apart to get their horses through," he said as he explained his ideas of how to structure such a fence.

Charlotte figured it was a good project to keep the men busy. She had Stormy to play with and she enjoyed taking walks around the beach with her. But the men seemed antsy and needed something to do. Working with their hands on a new project would be good for them.

The two of them decided to head into town with the Jamesons' wagon and pile what they could into it so they could start a good border fence around at least the front section of the property.

Charlotte watched them hitch up the horses and ride away. She was going to relax, when she realized that John had forgotten to grab the rifle. It was still propped against the barn where he'd set it while hitching the horses up. Normally that would not be a big deal. But with the town so deserted and Charlotte remembering how awful it was to be cornered by those renegade white men the month or so before, she just thought she would feel better if they had the gun.

She put Stormy in the house so she wouldn't follow her on the little journey, and then wrangled up her horse to throw a saddle and bridle on. She was soon on her way down the road, trotting so as to try to catch up with the wagon.

She could see them in the distance and soon gained on them enough to call out to them. Aaron slowed the horses and they turned around in their seats to watch her approach.

"Well look at that sight for sore eyes," John whistled as if he was seeing a woman for the very first time.

Aaron laughed and asked, "what's up, cowgirl? I thought you were leaving this task up to us men folk."

Charlotte giggled and felt relieved to see them in a good mood. Joking around had gone by the wayside for a while after the hurricane. Having a puppy helped and there was some laughter. But it was time for some more humor and smiles again.

"I figured I'd bring you this rifle you left, John," she said, hoisting it up to where he was sitting.

"Oh, thanks. I didn't even think about it after I set it down. I guess I'm getting too comfortable with the silence around town these days," he replied, setting the gun on the wagon floor by his feet.

She smiled, "I just wouldn't want anything to happen to you men."

Both of them smiled back and seemed to beam a little. Having a woman give them a little positive attention was not a bad thing. Charlotte hadn't felt up to flirting with either of them in a long time. It felt like a lifetime ago that she had spoken with Aaron about his feelings. And even longer ago that she was in John's arms. But it was starting to sound like something she might be interested in pursuing for the near future. A hobby, she laughed as she thought to herself. But she knew that she was just more and more lonely and the idea of someone holding her didn't sound like a bad idea, even if she was resisting such a thing before.

"Okay, well, are you coming along with us now or do you want to head back? It's up to you," Aaron asked.

"I could ride along for a little bit," she said. She didn't have anything else that was pressing at the moment. Seeing what debris John was talking about would be interesting. She let Hershel pace along with the wagon and she enjoyed the views of nature along the way. The fields were all grown up and wild now, without caretakers to mind the crops or to move livestock around. It was eerie, but also quite beautiful in the natural state.

They made it to the Lewis' farm- a smaller farm than the Jamesons' farm but with a much larger house. The big, southern porch was something Charlotte could only dream of owning someday. She imagined how the Lewis family used to sit on that porch with lemonade and watch the world go by. She wondered if they were doing okay in Key West. Did they make that arduous journey okay? Being used to an easy life must make a journey such as that much harder than it was for common folks like Andrew's family.

"Charlotte, can you stay with the horses while we scout out what's left behind the barn? I remember seeing a bunch of wood debris there- maybe from the shed they used to have back there that was half falling apart before the storm…" Aaron asked.

Charlotte nodded and jumped off Hershel. She reached for the reins to hold the other horses steady alongside her horse and prepared to wait around for a while.

But instead of waiting long, she watched as Aaron and John both came running back around the barn and hustled back to the wagon. "Get on your horse, Charlotte!" John called to her as they ran in her direction. "Get ready to go! Fast!"

She mounted her horse and watched them jump into the wagon and take off down the road. She galloped Hershel behind them, not sure why they were in such a hurry, but not willing to stay and find out.

They went around the bend in the road and ran the horses and wagon into the trees where the ground was packed hard enough to support the wheels. They were pretty much hidden from anything along the road. But she didn't understand why they were there.

"What's going on?" she asked, her voice strong and demanding but huffing and puffing a little from the excitement of the ride.

"We saw someone," John said.

"I think it was an Indian, scouting out the area," Aaron said. "Maybe he was just looking at the debris too. But it seemed like he was looking to see who was living there."

"Oh no," Charlotte gasped. "Do you think he saw you?"

Aaron and John looked at each other and then back to Charlotte. "I think he probably did," Aaron admitted. "He looked our direction. We jumped back behind the side of the barn as quick as we could. But he probably did see us."

"Could he see us ride away?" she asked.

They both shrugged. "He was back by the tree line behind the house when we saw him," Aaron explained. "If he saw us, he still wouldn't have had time to make it to the front of the barn before we were gone from view."

But Charlotte saw the way John looked at Aaron, as if he wasn't sure what Aaron said was the honest to God truth or if he was just wishfully thinking.

"We have to get back. Now." Charlotte demanded, turning her horse towards the road and then racing Hershel down the path as fast as she could get him to run.

She could only imagine what would happen if the man they saw was one of those Natives who was angry about the relocation efforts of the military. They would not be thrilled with anyone working for the United States government. Like, for example, the Lighthouse Service. She shuddered to think that they would try to harm them.

She wanted to get back before anyone could get inside. Her dog was in there. And if she and the men were able to get home, maybe they could still barricade the station enough to buy them more time.

When Aaron and John made it back to the property, they drove the wagon directly into the barn and then released the horses in the pasture and ran inside the house.

"I really hope the man you saw was part of Mica's tribe," Charlotte said, thinking that maybe there was a reason they didn't actually leave the area and were looking for supplies to get them through the season without trading with the townsfolk who were gone.

"I've never seen that man in my life," John said, hanging his head. "I am pretty sure it was someone from somewhere else."

"Are you sure it was an Indian?" she asked.

They both nodded. "He was dressed in something like what the Mayaimi wore and he had long hair, possibly tied back with something," John explained.

"Damn it," Charlotte muttered. "Damn, damn, damn."

The men stared at her.

"I'm sorry," she said. "I know I never swear. But this is scary as hell."

They both agreed.

"I don't even know what to do now. What do we do?" she started pacing the floor.

John let Stormy out of the bedroom and the dog ran around at their feet.

"I think we need to hide," Aaron said. "This light station is a sure target. We can stay somewhere in the woods nearby. Charlotte, don't you know of some places Mica took you to, that we could bed down at and still be able to keep close enough to light so we could get back whenever we can? Maybe if we keep the light lit, the troops will see it and come by eventually. No one has checked on the light station in so long. They are bound to come by soon. And then if we can last long enough without being discovered, maybe we can come back here when the Indians leave the area…"

Charlotte could tell he was thinking aloud. But it sounded like a good plan. "Okay. Yes, I do know a place. Mica used to take me to this place along the creek about a mile from here. It's deep in the woods and yet we could still come back here as needed to get more supplies or check on the light."

"That sounds like a good plan," John agreed. "Let's get some things together and then ride out there right away."

Charlotte found a rope for Stormy and tied it around her neck so she wouldn't wander off as they traveled. The men gathered the horses again and tied them to the hitching post. Then they all grabbed some food items and crammed them in packs. They stuck extra blankets under them in the saddles and threw coats on in case the night got chilly like the nights had been getting recently. "Let's get out of here quickly," Aaron advised. And they mounted the horses and Charlotte led them through a path along the back part of the property line and into the trees.

They found the lean-to building that Mica had shown Charlotte years before. It was more decrepit than she remembered, but it would work for a shelter for a few nights until things calmed down.

The men went about setting up a camp. They couldn't light a fire, because that would surely alert the Natives that they were there. But they piled the blankets together. No use worrying about proper etiquette at that point- they would need to stay close to keep warm during the nights without another heating source. They broke open a jar of beans and some fresh bread Charlotte had baked the day before and ate some lunch. It was somber at their makeshift campsite, but they felt safer out there than in the light station. They sat quietly and tried to enjoy the view of the creek next to the shack. But no one could truly relax.

"I wonder if they've found our house yet," Charlotte commented.

"I hope not," Aaron said. He went down to the water and rinsed their dinner plates while John drew something with a stick in the dirt and stared into the woods.

"I sure hope they are heading in a completely different direction," John said.

Charlotte and Aaron nodded.

"We'll see," Aaron said. "We'll see…"

Chapter Fourteen

It was a long day of just staying put and hoping the light station would be safe. Hours went by so slowly and they found little things to keep them occupied. John scouted further into the trees to find alternative paths for escape if the Seminole were to find their camp. Aaron tried fishing in the river with a string he pulled off of one of the sacks, tied around some worms he dug up along the creek bed. He occasionally yelled about catching something, but the fish were skilled at stealing the bait.

Charlotte played with Stormy and worked on rearranging the food supplies, over and over. There was nothing else to do. She yearned to go back home and settle back into the comforts of her normal surroundings.

Eventually it was supper time and they finished the rest of the beans and bread, and Charlotte pulled out some dried pork and they ate some of that too.

"I am going to have to sneak back over to the light station soon," she said, putting words to something they were all worrying about. "I need to keep it lit."

The men nodded and scuffed their boots in the dirt anxiously.

"I think I can run up there and at least light the wick and pull the curtains so the light can shine. I won't stay to actually polish everything or make things pretty," she said.

"That's a good idea," Aaron replied. "I agree, you shouldn't spend any extra time over there. Go in, and then get out quickly."

John nodded. "I could go instead," he suggested.

Charlotte adamantly said no.

"I could take the rifle and if anyone confronted me, I could shoot them," he continued.

"No, John. No way. That's my job and I will do it and hurry back. I can be fast and I am better than you are at staying hidden. Besides, if I get ambushed, you two can stay in the woods so you can help get me out of there," she insisted.

"She's right," Aaron agreed. "I think she will be the fastest of all of us at getting things done in the light tower. And we can make sure the coast is clear for her."

John shrugged. "I don't like having her in harm's way."

"None of us do," Aaron scoffed. "I would not agree for her to go if I didn't think it was our best chance at staying out of trouble."

Charlotte put her hand on his hand, and he squeezed it. "Thanks, Aaron. John, I promise I will be okay. But let's go see what the place looks like before we make any real efforts at getting into that tower. I just hope no one has beat us to it…"

They nodded.

"Let's tie Stormy up out here and hope she is quiet enough to keep from attracting the tribe out here. Then we can ride the horses part of the way and then walk the rest."

They cleaned up the mess from supper and started putting the plan into action.

Stormy seemed worried about them leaving but she was not a big barker. She spun around a few times on her leash then laid back down to wait as they left her sight. The horses picked through the bushes and when they were about three hundred feet from the property line, they tied them up to some trees and started walking the rest of the way as planned.

They found a nice overlook area where they could see most of the property and the beach. They waited for several minutes to watch for any movement or anything out of ordinary. But nothing caught their attention.

"I think it's okay," Charlotte said finally. "I'm going to go."

Aaron nodded. "Just use whatever kerosene is up there, Charlotte. Don't go trying to fill the tank or anything that will take too much time. Light the wicks and then get out."

She agreed. "I'll be really fast and really cautious, don't worry."

John had a crease across his forehead. "I'm still not thrilled about this," he confessed. "Be careful."

Charlotte walked over to him and pulled him into her arms for a big hug. "I know you're worried, John. But I will be right back. It will be fine."

He pulled back from her arms and gave her a tiny kiss, his lips barely brushing her cheekbone. "Okay," he said, then let her go. She was tempted to just stay there, in the comfort of those big arms forever. She could feel his tension when they touched and knew he probably felt the same. If they could only just skip the lighthouse tasks and just run off into the woods and be safe and never have to worry again, she would love to make that choice. But, she knew her brother was counting on her if he was out there somewhere. And all the other ship captains at sea. Plus, being in the woods was likely even more dangerous. So, they had no choice.

Without another glance backwards, she left the men and silently crept through the grass at the edge of the property and then made a mad dash for the light tower door.

John and Aaron scanned the area for any movement or any reactions from the environment. But nothing changed. Some birds flew away from the clothesline next to the house when she ran through, but no one seemed to be watching the house except them.

She turned to look at them before pushing the door open. They nodded in her direction. Go ahead.

She ran as fast as she could up the stairs. From the top of the lighthouse she had a broad view of the area around the light station and a little view into the forest beyond. She scanned the region quickly, and not seeing anything interesting she grabbed three new wicks and prepared them as fast as she'd ever prepared wicks before. Then she put them into the lantern and struck a match, lighting them quickly and carefully. She knew now was the most dangerous moment of all, because the huge light would come to light and refract 20 miles out to sea as it spun on its axis through the glass panels.

She threw the rest of the matchbook down on the little countertop and took one last look at the burning light to make sure it didn't burn out. Then she rushed back down the stairs, out the door, and across the grass to where John and Aaron stood with their eyes on their scopes, ready to fire if needed. Then they all turned and rushed through the bushes, back to their horses and took off down the path toward their temporary quarters.

They didn't relax or slow down until they were back at the edge of the creek, being greeted by a rambunctious German Shepherd puppy.

"Oh, wow. We did it," Charlotte said, taking deep breaths and trying to calm her racing heartbeats.

"You did it," John smiled. "That was so quick, and the light was lit and then you were out of there."

Aaron smiled, "That was great. It's amazing how fast you can do that job when you need to hurry. You're a professional," he said. "Funny how long it takes you on a normal day."

"Ha. Funny," she grinned back. "It's a little more involved when I actually want to do it well and when I'm not worried about being shot at by Indians from the tree line."

They all laughed nervously. It was only half funny because it was so true. At any point they could be sitting ducks for Natives or renegades who would gladly shoot at them.

"Now we have to do it again in the morning to turn off the light," she reminded them.

They all grimaced. It was going to be an ongoing stress. Either way, they were going to have to live with this fear every day to take care of the light, or eventually they might have to actually face an invasion. Neither option sounded fun, but there was still a chance that no one would show up at the light. It was a slim chance, but Charlotte figured that thinking about there being any chance at all that they could make it through this ordeal until Andrew returned was the only way she could keep her sanity while they waited.

They settled onto their blankets as the sun put on a beautiful show for them with orange and pinks and reds and even some purple above the treetops.

John was the first to get to sleep, with Aaron agreeing to take the first watch. Aaron set up his blanket on the ground outside the shed door and Charlotte went to sit with him. John didn't waste any time in hitting the pillow and starting to snore.

"You sure you want a man like that?" Aaron laughed. "He sounds like a bear with a broken snout when he sleeps."

Charlotte giggled and leaned into Aaron's wide chest to use it as a makeshift pillow. Aaron welcomed her with his arms wide and he propped himself up against the side of the shed.

"Oh, Aaron, I am glad you stayed with me and didn't go to Key West or to the Bahamas yet," she said.

He nodded. "Me too. Who knows what would have happened in Key West anyway."

Charlotte agreed. They still had no idea who survived the storm or who may not have. They had no news and now they had no way of getting into town and checking the telegraph news. She sighed. "Yes, and if you'd gone, I would have missed you."

He hugged her against his chest. She felt safe there. She glanced back at the door and could still hear the snoring. She was glad John wasn't awake to interpret the situation incorrectly or get upset because of his own expectations and hopes about her.

"When you leave," Charlotte continued, "where will you go? Are you still planning on trying to cross over to the Bahamas even with all of the chaos here?"

Aaron nodded. "I need to, Charlotte," he said. "I don't know if I told you the story before, Charlotte. I was afraid you might feel obligated to tell Andrew and that would have been tragic…"

"What is it? And why would you ever think I would tell Andrew anything that might be problematic for you? You're my best friend."

He shrugged. "Sometimes the dynamics of the world mean that we can't really be best friends completely," he said. "Sometimes the risk of telling anyone something is outweighed by the risk of ruining something much more important."

She raised her eyebrows, more interested now in whatever he was trying to say. "Okay," she agreed. "What story, Aaron?"

"When I was young and working as a slave in Georgia, I heard stories about this Underground Railroad thing. It was a network of people who were working to help slaves escape to non-slave areas. They moved the people from place to place in the night and kept them hidden in the days. And eventually they could get them to the areas where the Southern soldiers couldn't find them or make them return."

Charlotte listened intently. "I remember hearing about that, too. But I also heard that the slaves in the South were out of luck because that Underground Railroad was operating in the northern areas and those around Georgia weren't close enough."

"That was true, but eventually they put together a southern route. They called it the Saltwater Underground Railroad. It was put together to take slaves to the beaches of Florida and then onto boats that took them to British-owned Bahama islands. The location where they loaded the boats was right here where the light station is."

Her eyes widened. "I knew you said some people had traveled to the Bahamas from here. And Mica told me something about that too. But I had no idea it was so extensive," she said. Then she turned around to look him in the eyes directly, realizing why he was telling her this. "You've been helping them, haven't you?"

He didn't answer at first. "I have done what I could."

"Wow," she gasped. "That sounds very dangerous. And yet, all I can think is that I wish I knew so I could help too."

"Well, Charlotte, I know you mean that you would have liked to do that. I know you like to think that. But in reality, you could never have done such a thing. Your loyalty was to your brother and the light station. The Saltwater Underground was a direct threat to your safety and that of his family. That's why we had to do it without anyone knowing. Especially anyone at the light station itself. And anyway, we couldn't continue to do anything as often when things started getting more dangerous and Andrew's family moved into the new lighthouse and you came here…"

"So, you didn't do it once the light was built?" she asked.

"We tried. But it was harder. The whole bay was lit up with the light. So, we had to work out of the other Keys mostly. It has been challenging to say the least."

"I had no idea," she whispered. "I can't believe all that was happening, and I didn't even have a clue."

"I know," he said. "That was how it was designed."

"That's why you want to go to the Bahamas?" she asked. "That's where other slaves went? Is that how your family got there?"

He pulled her shoulders so that she was tightly against his chest in a big hug. "Yes, Charlotte. That's how they got about six thousand slaves out of the South. That's how they got my family out. And that's where I was heading when I found your brother and he convinced me to stay for a while with him so I could save up enough money to help them. Every spare dime he's paid me has been saved for getting them there safely, and to help them survive there. And it also meant

I could stay on this side of the sea and help get more people out, longer."

She could see his eyes gleaming in the twilight. "That's amazing, Aaron," she whispered. "You're amazing."

Sitting in his arms in the dark was magical. It wasn't the fireworks and electricity that she got when John touched her. But it was a deep friendship, safe kind of feeling. She was afraid out there in the trees, and she wished she was home safely in her bed. But at the same time, she was thankful for this special moment with her great friend.

"I'm excited for you, Aaron," she told him. "Your family must be so proud of you."

"Thank you," he whispered back, hugging her even more. "Thanks for being such a good friend to me, Charlotte. Thanks for always trying to make things better when life has been pretty hard for us all."

She laughed, "Aaron, I never had to TRY to do anything. I just do what my heart tells me. And I've always enjoyed being your friend. I'm really going to miss you when you're gone."

"Yeah," he said. "I will miss you a lot too."

They sat in the dark, silently, listening to the crickets and the rushing creek and the beating of each other's hearts. It was going to be a long night and a stressful morning. She was thankful for their time together and even more so, aware of the value of limited time.

Chapter Fifteen

The sun finally crested over the trees, and they started moving around. John had taken the last watch, so he was already awake and preparing some breakfast out of a mishmash of containers they had thrown in the bag. Without a fire it made it impossible to cook anything. No bacon and eggs today. Instead, they found some granola mix and a couple of the oranges that were picked at the end of the season from the trees in the light station yard.

It was time to run over and extinguish the lighthouse lamp. If the sun were to shine just right through the glass of the Fresnel lens, it could start fires on the land wherever it shined. Like using a magnifying glass to start a smoldering pile of dry leaves. And they really couldn't afford to waste any lamp oil by leaving the lamp lit during the daylight hours.

"I have to get over to the light station to close the curtains and extinguish the flames," she said.

"We figured you'd be in a rush," Aaron said. "We're ready to go with you whenever you're ready."

Charlotte pet Stormy and tied her back up like the last time. The dog was more distressed about the situation than before. "What's the matter, Stormy?" she asked, petting her course fur. "We'll be right back." But Stormy was whining and pacing back and forth.

"What's wrong with the puppy?" John asked, noticing the change in behavior.

"I'm not sure. She may just realize we are leaving her since we didn't come back for a little bit last time," Charlotte guessed.

"I'm not sure…" Aaron said, quietly. "Maybe she senses something." He walked slowly down the path a short distance and then just as slowly and quietly back. He motioned his finger to his lips to keep them all silent.

"Do you hear or see anything?" Charlotte asked when he was back at her side.

"I can't tell if anything is different. But dogs know things we don't know. Let's just stay absolutely silent when we head over there, just in case."

They agreed and quietly moved towards the horses and led them on foot down the path until they were beyond a thicket of palm fronds. Then they hoisted themselves up and rode for a distance before hopping back off, this time a little farther from the light station than before.

"Let's approach on foot, just in case there's something going on that requires us to be sneakier," Aaron suggested.

"I think we should split up and walk around the perimeter of the property on each side. We can meet back here after Charlotte takes care of the light. But before she goes up there, we should make sure things are clear," John said.

"Good plan," Aaron replied. "I have a weird feeling about things right now. The dog sensed it, and now I do too. The birds are too quiet. There are likely people somewhere close by. Let's proceed with caution even more than before."

Charlotte bit her lip and looked around nervously. She didn't know whether to truly be afraid if the intruders could be Seminoles. What if they were with Mica and her family? What if they just needed help?

But on the other hand, she knew there were bands of Natives who were going around causing havoc and burning farms down. Some even killed whole families on the other side of the Intercoastal Waterway. That was why so many people decided to go to Key West. Knowing the other townsfolk were scared and that there were really murderous Natives anywhere around there, she knew she should also be worried at least to some degree. Plus, Mica told her that she should leave...

Charlotte felt her heart beat quicken. She hoped that if someone was around the area who wasn't supposed to be there, that they weren't there to do anything too dangerous or to cause any damage to the light station. And if anything did happen, she hoped that they could chase them away.

Aaron and John had their rifles cocked and aimed in front of them as they each walked a different direction around the light station yard. Charlotte stayed back, waiting for them to give her the signal that it was all clear.

But it didn't come.

Instead, John started motioning wildly, waving his hands in the air and pointing all around them. As he did,

Charlotte followed his gaze and could see what he saw. There were Seminoles in the oak trees and even the orange trees. There were Seminoles standing in the shadows all around them. There were Seminoles everywhere. And they had noticed Aaron and John walking around and were already shooting at them.

Charlotte wasn't sure where the guns came from. Most of the Natives in the area hunted with bows and arrows and only used guns for absolute necessity, like when the wild pig got into the camp and had attacked some of the women a couple of years ago. Mica's tribe had guns that they received in trade for fish and other things that they traded with the townsfolk. But they didn't have enough rifles to outfit a large group like this one.

These are not Mica's tribes' people, she realized. Or if some of them were from her tribe, there were also many who were not. These were the Natives that they'd heard about. The ones who were so angry at the whites for the removal policies and they were not there to trade or to talk with them. They were there to kill them.

The Natives were already shooting buckshot and rifle balls towards Aaron and John.

Her scream was caught in her throat as she watched her friends scramble to find cover and she was unable to do anything from where she hid.

At one point it looked as if they'd both been hit- she thought maybe in the legs, but she realized that Aaron may have taken a hit in his shoulder too. She saw his arm jerk back and stumble. But then they got up and both kept running. They were running to the light tower. It was their only chance to get inside a shelter from where they were.

Charlotte had to decide what to do to give Aaron and John a chance to make it the remaining distance without getting shot more. She only had one opportunity to do something, or it would be too late.

She jumped out of the woods and started yelling to the Natives in a broken dialect mixture of English and that of the Mayaimi- Seminole language. "I am Charlotte," she started, her voice strong and unwavering. "We are friends. We are Mayaimi friends."

The gunshots ceased as the Natives paused to look her direction. They looked confused for a minute and they looked around at each other and towards John and

Aaron who were running as they realized what she was doing to give them some time.

One who seemed to be leading the group, yelled to the others. Charlotte could not understand what he said. He pointed at her. Several of them rushed towards her, rifles aimed her direction. The others resumed their attack on John and Aaron who were almost to the tower.

She put up her hands to show she was unarmed and not dangerous. One of them, a thin man with a young face and his hair shaved on top and only a ponytail in the back, grabbed one of her hands roughly and spun her around. He held her tightly against him and marched her out of the clearing and behind the keepers' cottage where he forced her to sit on the ground. He kept glaring at her and then speaking quickly with the other men who were standing with him, with their rifles focused on her head.

Charlotte didn't care that they were rough with her, nor that they pointed guns at her. She knew if they wanted to kill her, they would have already done so. They must be saving her to keep as a hostage or to take her somewhere. Whatever they planned, she hoped she had at least bought her friends some time. She couldn't see what was going on anymore. But she soon could see smoke coming from above the cottage where she knew the light tower stood.

She hoped that meant that John and Aaron were okay and that they started a fire to bring attention to the island. Maybe someone somewhere would see the fire and come help them.

It seemed like forever as she heard more shooting and a lot of yelling. And then it got really quiet for a few minutes.

One of the Seminole cried out and she heard a mad rush of footsteps.

Then there was a boom so loud that Charlotte's ears stopped working. There was a ringing and everything seemed to be in slow motion. She realized there had been an explosion so loud that it knocked her backwards into the grass and blew the wind out of her lungs.

What had blown up? She started focusing her thoughts but everything still seemed to be spinning.

Where were John and Aaron? She wanted to run over to find them and see what was going on, but she knew the Natives would kill her before she could even take three steps. They all were blown back from the blast too, but recovered quickly and held the guns back on her. And then several of them were grabbing her and forcing her to her feet.

"My dog," she whispered. But no one listened. Where was Stormy? She hoped Stormy was okay where she was. She hoped she could get back to her before too long. If she was able to chew through her rope, she hoped she would hide from the loud noises and find somewhere safe. She would have to try to find her later.

Someone said something in Seminole that again Charlotte could barely understand, but his hand motions made it clear he meant to come with them. They marched her into the brush and for what seemed like a long time down a path she didn't recognize- maybe a path they had created when they came to the light station last night or that morning.

She was picked up and forced onto one of their ponies. It was hard to tell where she was on the island at that point. She was turned around and still reeling from the effects of the explosion. But they tied her hands to the ropes on the makeshift saddle. Then they got on the other horses and galloped away, with the horse Charlotte was on dragging behind. She bounced painfully on the horses' back as they ran for what seemed like forever.

"My dog," she tried to call to them. "Where is my dog? You can't take me away. I need to find her…"

But no one responded or even seemed to care as her voice drifted away in the wind. They continued to ride fast through the trees.

Where were they taking her? She had no idea what they planned to do with her. Would John and Aaron be able to find her? She had no idea what happened to them when the explosion happened. She hoped they were the ones who lit the explosion on purpose. It must have been the kerosene tank, or maybe some gunpowder that they stored in the light tower. She had no idea what happened or what she should even fear. She just hoped they could find her. She had no way to leave a trail, but the horses were leaving an indent in the grass and bushes. Maybe they could follow that to find her.

She continued bobbing along on the horse until they came to a spot on the Intercoastal waterway where they had apparently stashed many canoes. They pulled her from the horse and into one of the boats. Then they pushed off into the waterway, pulling the horses into the waves to swim behind them as they crossed the channel.

Charlotte could taste the seawater spraying at her as they held her down on the floor of the canoe. It made her think of Andrew and Catharine and their kids and the other townspeople on the last day she saw any of them when they crossed the water and disappeared from her view. She felt tears gather behind her eyelids. But she wouldn't cry. She couldn't cry. She needed to stay strong and make it through this situation so she could go back and find John and Aaron.

But were they even still alive?

She imagined them hurt and suffering and that made it even harder to accept that she was a hostage. She fought the straps they'd tied on her hands and wiggled, trying to flop out of the canoe. But one of the Seminole noticed her actions and slapped her side with the butt of his rifle. The sting rang through her nerves, up her spine. She screamed out, "no!" and winced, moving away from him as he threatened to hit her again with it.

She was stuck. There was nothing she could do yet. But she was determined to find a way out of there and back to John and Aaron.

When they made it across the water, they again forced her onto the back of a pony.

She was dragged what seemed like for hours through the swamplands. They were taking her into the Everglades. She imagined all the ways they could kill her out there and no one would ever find her body. They could feed her to the snakes or the alligators or the panthers. There were so many ways to die in the Everglades. She shivered thinking of them all and resolved to be as calm and compliant as possible until she knew what they planned to do with her.

Chapter Sixteen

The journey finally seemed to be coming to an end. The Seminole slowed the horses and led her to a clearing where she could see makeshift tents and structures hidden in the reeds and palms. Other Natives were coming out to greet them and the horses whinnied to other horses that were tied up in a corral area.

It was apparently their home, if you could call it a home. It was a camp, and a well-hidden one, at that. The tents blended into the tans and greens of the grasses and palms. It was now even more clear to Charlotte that the rumors were true- that the U.S. troops struggled to find the Seminole hideouts… that they felt like they were constantly having to protect themselves from attacks from a foe they could not even see. It was amazing how well they camouflaged their homes in the thickest areas of the jungle out there in the Everglades.

She had no idea how far they had traveled that day, but she figured it was at least eight to ten hours. Her muscles ached and she was scorched from the sun. Luckily, part way into the journey they had covered her head with a large hat, woven from palm fronds. They also put something on her face that kept her from burning up completely. Maybe it was aloe or something like that. It felt refreshing on her skin. A little tingly too.

She knew she could be dead if the Natives wanted her dead. They all could be. She wondered if John and Aaron were able to get out of the light tower and hide somewhere. Maybe they were also overheated and hungry. Maybe they were able to slip away in the water and hide in a cove somewhere. That would be much more refreshing than traveling all day in the Florida heat like she had been forced to do.

Ugh, she was so done with riding horses. She took a deep breath, trying to re-center her thoughts that were reeling in her mind.

They dragged her down from the saddle and she tumbled forward, almost losing her footing from her muscles being so achy and weak. She was a horseback rider, but not an all-day horseback rider. This was way more riding than she had ever done in a day, and her body rebelled against the idea of moving at all now.

The same pony-tailed man who had thrown her to the ground when they first captured her, now pushed her forward down a path towards one of the canvas structures. She stumbled to the entrance, and he pointed to make her go in.

He spoke in what sounded like Seminole with someone in the darkness beyond and there were several responses that she could not understand. She made out the word "friend," and "Mayiami," Maybe something about a battle and shooting, but she mostly interpreted that from the hand signals the man was making to explain the story. He was likely telling them about the battle at the lighthouse. And about her.

Her eyes adjusted to the darkness better and she could see she was surrounded by Natives who were sitting against the sides of the tent and walking around. She didn't recognize the main speakers.

One of them stepped outside the tent and called to someone else. Charlotte immediately recognized the man who appeared from around the corner of the path and entered the tent. Mica called him Chittee Yholo, which she said stood for The Snake That Makes a Noise. He was Mica's older cousin who was rumored to be an up-and-coming chief of the tribe.

"Chittee?" she said, raising her hand in greeting."

"No," he glared. "I am not Chittee now," he corrected her. "They call me Billy."

Charlotte smiled nervously, "Billy, I'm so glad to see you. Is Mica here?"

Billy continued glaring. "Why are you here? Why did you stay and not go with your people?" he demanded.

"I needed to keep the lighthouse working," she said. "I promised I would take care of the light and the station." It sounded silly now, she realized. She would have been better off staying with her family and friends. Now she was here, wherever that was, and even Billy seemed very upset.

He was not the friendly man she met when she and Mica were bugging him to let them go fishing with him, or when he was trading his leather goods and they were trying to weave the leather he had left over. It was a totally different situation. Charlotte could tell he was not pleased to see her there.

"You were foolish," he quipped. "You are lucky Natto recognized you and brought you here. They would have killed you," he motioned to the ponytailed man who had brought her there.

She was surprised to hear that the man had recognized her. She didn't remember Natto. But she knew Mica's tribe was bigger than just the people she saw regularly when she and Mica hung out together.

Charlotte swallowed and felt the lump that was building in her throat. "What did they do with my friends John and Aaron?" she asked.

Billy waved as if to say, "never mind," and then he motioned for her to follow him.

She complied, each step painful as she made her way next to him, through the back of the tent, through a thicket of rushes and to the edge of a creek.

She recognized several of the other men and women who gathered closer when they saw her there.

One of the women stood aside and let someone push their way to the front of the crowd. Charlotte instantly recognized Mica, even though her hair was cut very short now and she was wearing black-striped paint on her face, framing her eyes.

"Mica," she called out.

"Charlotte. You made a big mistake," Mica shook her head. "I told you not to stay there. I told you to go to Key West."

Charlotte nodded, "I know," she said, hanging her head. "I had to keep the lighthouse going for Andrew."

Mica kept shaking her head. "They want to kill you, Charlotte. They've talked about killing you."

Charlotte felt that lump grown in her throat.

"Will they?" she asked quietly.

"I told them you are my friend," Mica said. "But your people, the white men, are killing our family. The tribe does not care that you were a friend before. They said you will kill us too if we don't kill you now."

"You know that isn't true," Charlotte gasped and plead with Mica's eyes silently… *We were friends, Mica. We were friends!* She knew she could not speak the words but they were there between them in the darkness.

"I don't know anything," Mica said, staring her in the eyes. "You are a white woman. You care about your white soldiers. You are not Mayiami. You are not Seminole. You are the enemy."

Charlotte felt the tears run into her eyes and felt like she had been slapped. This was not the same Mica. She must have seen some hard things and probably knew much more than Charlotte knew. Charlotte knew there was much more than what she was aware of. Being at the lighthouse with the townspeople gone meant she did not hear much news anymore, except the occasional report about the hurricane damage that John had told her.

She wondered what else John had heard that he didn't share with her...

"I didn't go to Key West because I wanted to make sure you were okay," Charlotte tried to explain. But she realized how feeble her thoughts were- how immature and naïve she had been. The Mayiami didn't need her help. Mica's tribe was running a whole war defensive and Charlotte was merely just an annoyance. She was in the way.

"I didn't want anything to happen to you, Mica. I know now how little I understood about the war and the conflicts. But I did what I could to make sure the townspeople who could have been more dangerous left and went to Key West and didn't stay to harm you..."

Mica turned a blind eye towards her words. "Charlotte, you are in danger."

"I understand that more now," Charlotte said, sensing so many eyes on them as they stood there. It was no longer her and Mica but her against a whole tribe who were on-edge because of serious threats to their lives and their livelihood.

But she knew this was her only opportunity to find out more about her friends so she took a chance at asking, "I am also worried about John Thompson and Aaron Carter. They were with me at the light station. They didn't mean any harm to anyone. They were just trying to work on the light to help me. And I don't know what happened to them."

Mica scoffed. "White men. I do not know of your friends. But if they were discovered by the warriors, they are likely dead now. They do not leave white men alive. Just as the white men do not leave our family alive."

Charlotte felt a blanket of doom envelop her as she realized Mica was probably right.

"I need to go back and see," she said, a new level of panic setting in. She tried to mask her anxiousness but her words betrayed her. "Please, Mica. Please. I need to know. And if they were able to get away, I need to find them. Or perhaps if they did die, I need to bury them." Her voice trailed off.

"Charlotte," Mica said, "you cannot go back there."

"I need to."

"You will be killed."

Charlotte shrugged. "It is worse to live and not know."

"You've always done things that people say not to do." Charlotte could see a little piece of the old Mica showing through the armor.

She forced a small smile.

Mica nodded, "I will talk to Billy. Maybe I can ask him if you could stay with me when he leaves again."

Charlotte returned the nod and she looked at the strong warrior woman in front of her. "Please try."

"I will try." Mica walked back out of the clearing and the other Seminole who were standing nearby and staring out of curiosity also walked away.

The man who Billy called Natto came and took her arm and led her back inside the tent and made her sit down. Another Seminole man stood by the entrance of the tent, motioning her to stay where she was and not move.

She waited for Billy to return after he left, but the minutes ticked by, and he didn't come back.

She leaned against something that felt like a tree stump and felt her eyes getting heavier and heavier. The light outside changed to dusk and her eyes closed.

I will just take a little break to rest my eyes, she thought. But after all the journeying and stress she couldn't stop herself from falling fast asleep.

Chapter Seventeen

Charlotte woke to the tip of a sharp object sticking in her side. "Ouch, stop!" she called out, rubbing the sleep out of her eyes.

She saw Natto standing over here, blocking the sunlight that was streaming into the tent now. It must be evening; the sun was very low but still hot on her face.

"Come," he motioned. It was the first English word she had heard come from his mouth.

She let him help her to her feet.

"Now go," he said, pushing her out into the clearing.

"Wait, what?" she asked. "I have no idea where I am now. You can't just kick me out. Other Natives will try to kill me. Or snakes. Or gators."

He shrugged, obviously not understanding her words. Or, perhaps understanding enough and not caring.

"Where is Mica?" she asked, trying to stop him from shoving her into the brambles that led to what appeared to be another pathway.

"Wait, please. Find Mica…" her voice drifted away.

She heard some leaves rustle and she looked up and saw Mica walking up the path with her horse.

"Hershel!" she called out and ran to Mica's side where she took the reins from her hands. "Thank you! How did you find him?"

Mica half smiled back at her, understanding her love for her horse. But she stiffened up again. "You must go," she insisted. "You will die here. Go before they change their minds."

"But it is going to be dark. I have no idea where to go."

She shrugged. "You have better chances in the Glades than you have here."

Charlotte realized there was no changing their minds. She dropped her head and took a step forward with Hershel's reins.

"Wait," Mica said, pulling her aside near a tree where no one else could see her for a second. "I grabbed some things for you." She pointed at the bag on the back of the saddle pad. "A blanket. Some food for at least one or two meals. A knife." She looked around and her voice was almost a whisper at the end of that sentence. "I need you to take it and go, quickly. They will be very mad I gave you those things. I tied them under the saddle so they would not notice. When you get far enough away from here, then you can take them out before you get on the horse."

Charlotte nodded. "Thank you, Mica."

Mica's mouth tightened for a second.

"I hope you stay safe. I miss you already," Charlotte whispered to her old friend as she started leading her horse away.

Mica was not the same. Neither of them was anymore. No one was. The times they were in were changing everything. She yearned for the old days when they could run around on the beaches and in the forest and no one cared that they were friends. The days when they ran in and out of each other's homes and knew each other's families. Now, they could not be each other's families anymore. Mica made it clear they could not even be friends.

Charlotte paused one more time and turned back. "Mica?" she asked. "Do you know anything about Key West? Have you heard anything from your tribe about the hurricane down there?"

Mica shook her head. "No." She looked down. "I did hear it was very bad. Many people were killed." Then, as if she remembered the same things Charlotte was thinking about from their youth, she added, "I hope your family is okay."

Charlotte nodded. "Thank you. I hope so too." She turned away at that point, no longer able to keep a stoic face with so many emotions circling. She took her horse and they started walking away, leaving the temporary camp and heading out into the darkening jungle beyond.

They walked for several minutes until she could no longer hear the Seminole talking behind her and no longer smelled their campfires. Then she loosened the cinch on the heavy, leather saddle and pushed it to the side. The items Mica told her about were there. She took the sack and tied it around her waist with the rope Mica used to tie it to the saddle. She couldn't imagine how she would have survived the Everglades without those things. It would be hard enough without a fire tonight to scare the creepy things away. She shuddered just imagining what animals were watching her now, as she got back on Hershel and they walked in the shadows.

The sun was going down and the jungle marshland came even more alive around her. She heard the crickets in the grass and the rustling of the reeds. There were screams that she hoped were just the screeching of owls in the distance… and maybe the other crying noises were just frog calls.

She could see dark objects darting in the air around her, which she figured were bats catching insects. There was a thunderstorm out there somewhere, shaking the place with a low rumbling, and she worried it could rain soon if that storm came her way. Even though she had spent a lifetime with Florida thunder and lightning, after the recent hurricane she was much more nervous about the winds and rain.

I need to hunker down somewhere for the night, she thought. *I have no idea where I am going or where I should be going, and I will end up leading Hershel into the water or getting chased by an alligator.* The thought of those giant gators or the venomous snakes made her shiver. *I am going to die here*, she sighed. *I should have stayed hidden at the light station and then I could be there with John and Aaron now. They must think I'm dead. Ugh... maybe they are hurt or dying, or even dead...* but she knew she couldn't think that way. It made her freeze up and not be able to think about anything else.

She decided to stop and eat some food and let Hershel graze. She dropped to the ground and led him over to a tree on the top of a clearing in the path that seemed to have more elevation than the surrounding areas. Water glistened in the moonlight beyond a short stretch of bushes and trees as she tied the horse with enough room to snack on the grass around his feet.

The gators would probably be over there by the water, she told herself. But she knew gators were all over the region. And the snakes. And the spiders. And rats. And Florida panthers. She would have to sleep lightly if she could even sleep at all that night.

She collected some palm fronds from the scrub palmetto bushes and some branches that had fallen from the trees. It was almost too dark to forage for supplies, but she needed something to protect her. It would at least give her some peace of mind to know that the creatures would have to transverse some fronds in order to eat her.

She started building a makeshift fort. She was tempted to gather some of the soft Spanish moss that had fallen from the trees, but she knew it would need to be cleaned or the mites would infest her area and cause her to itch and be bit up for days.

She decided to just use the little blanket that Mica sent with her. It was woven from tough yarn and would give her at least some protection from the dew that would surely cover her by morning.

She checked Hershel's ties again and then sat down to snack on the nuts and berries that Mica had packed for her. She was thirsty but would wait until morning to try to seek something to drink. She didn't want to end up fighting with a gator to get to the water. Plus, she would have to find a spring or a flowing creek. The Everglades water near the coast was brackish and would make her sick.

That was, IF she was near the coast. She had no idea. And no idea how she would figure that out, either.

She finished her handful of food and decided to save the rest for tomorrow. She was still tired from her adventures. Even with a lot of sleep yesterday… or was it earlier today (her days were blurring together… time was not real now…) she was still ready to sleep.

She closed her eyes and prayed that she wouldn't wake to anything too crazy in the middle of the night.

Fortunately, she fell sound asleep almost immediately and slept straight through.

Chapter Eighteen

Her eyes jerked open when she heard Hershel snorting loudly in the morning sun. He must be thirsty, she realized.

Her tongue felt terribly parched against her dry lips. *Okay, time to find water…* she stood up and stretched. Her body still ached from the all-day horseback ride with Natto.

The path was much easier to follow during the daytime and she could see indents in the grass and bushes where she imagined animals must have slipped through to access the water. She knew she needed to explore a little before drinking anything. A stomachache or diarrhea could be deadly out here. She had no idea how long she would be stuck wandering before she could find any towns or other (safe) people.

She left Hershel and scooted through the brush towards the water she saw in the moonlight last night.

There were skid marks in the grass- probably where gators slid into the water. She decided to avoid that entrance for now and keep walking. A creek would be a better idea- that water wasn't moving much.

She saddled up and they were back on the trail again quickly. They followed the trail religiously, in case it actually would take them wherever the tribe had taken her from, earlier.

After what seemed like a long time, Charlotte heard what she had been listening for- the noise of flowing water along the reeds. She looked through the bushes and could see water glistening just beyond. She again left Hershel tied to a small tree and as he grazed, she headed towards the water, stepping carefully so as to avoid encountering anything scary.

This water was actually flowing. She wasn't sure where it came from or where it was headed, but it seemed to be flowing at least in the same direction she was walking. Which could mean they were heading towards the coast. She hoped it would be the coast near her island. But at this point she just needed something to drink.

She dipped her hands in the stream and put the

water near her nose. It didn't smell bad. She stuck her tongue in it. It didn't taste bad. She decided to risk it. She shoved her palms back into the flow and drank deeply. The water soothed the back of her throat and she continued to take a few hands full. She needed to let Hershel drink too. She went back up to the path and untied him.

He pushed his nose into the cool creek, seeming just as eager to drink as she had been, and she let him take a few drinks before stopping him and moving him back to the path. It wasn't a good idea for either of them to drink too much, especially if there were any contaminants.

They continued down the path.

The hours went by slowly. She entertained herself by watching the birds flee as they approached, and smiling as some of the smaller birds flitted from tree to bush to tree around them. She saw a couple of rabbits and a few turtles as they continued. But nothing too trecherous.

She knew the gators and snakes were watching her somewhere just beyond her sight, but she was happy that they stayed clear of her path. At one point she thought she saw a gator's tail disappear into the rushes before they got to the other side of a curve in the path. But she rushed Hershel through the area and didn't look too carefully, out of the fear of actually seeing it close enough to do anything to them. Her mind created so many scary situations, but she continued down the path all day long. She had no other choice and the idea of being stuck out there for another night was weighing heavily on her mind.

She found a clearing at some point that seemed familiar. Maybe it was where she had stopped with Natto and his crew when they gave her some jerky to eat and some water to drink before continuing on. She hoped she was still on the right track.

Sometimes the path seemed to be almost invisible. As she journeyed, she realized she was encountering the areas the Natives may have walked through even longer and longer ago. The indented parts that were fresher in the beginning of her trip yesterday were not as fresh now as she got further away from Mica's group. She had to trust that her horse remembered the way, and gave him his head more than tried to control him when there were any decisions to be made. He seemed confident enough about where they were going, and even more so as the day went on and they hopefully got closer to wherever the path was leading.

Of course, there was always a chance that the path was not really the Seminole's trail, and they were just going in circles. She strongly hoped that was not the case. But it was certainly possible.

When it started to get dark again, she realized that either they were lost… or they were not going fast enough to make the same time as what the Seminoles had been able to cover in a day, before. She wanted to keep pushing forward in case the latter was true. But she knew they would have to cross the water anyway. If they ever got to the water…

She repeated her actions from the night before. Although it was harder to find palm fronds in this marshier area. She found enough reeds to weave herself a rough mat to lay on and unrolled the blanket from around her waist.

She ate the last handful of nuts and berries and could hear her stomach growling for more. It would be a long day tomorrow without food. But at this point she didn't want to risk eating something that looked like food, such as some of the berries she had seen along the way. She just didn't know enough about this area. Mica would have known. And Mica had shown her a lot of things around their island. But wherever she was now could be different, and she didn't want to get sick or die now. She needed to get home.

She bedded down like before and Hershel munched on some grass around her. This time it was harder to fall asleep. She could hear the cries of some kind of larger mammal. She couldn't tell if it was a coyote or a wild cat. Whatever it was made her spine tingle and her heart catch. Please don't come over here, she thought.

But a few hours later she could hear something large in the bushes around her. Each footstep crunching around her made her want to cry out, but she held her breath carefully. She was sure that whatever it was could hear her breathing. Maybe it was looking for food nearby and she just thought it was stalking her little camp. But it was possible it just wanted to eat her. She tried to breathe shallowly and to not move on the rustley reed mat.

After what seemed like an hour, the footsteps retreated and she didn't hear it anymore.

There was no way she could sleep after that. She stared into the darkness, startling and freezing her muscles to be still yet again from every little noise around her.

She continued that pattern until the sun came up.

Then she and Hershel were back on the path, hurrying to reach the end, wherever that may take them.

Around what she figured was noon, she spotted a Y in the road and stopped the horse. What was this? She didn't remember a Y in the road. But, how could she? She had been tied up and following quickly on horseback if she came through this place with the Natives the other day. She easily could have missed directional differences.

Ugh. She was stuck. If she went one way, she might end up on the right path towards the shore where she could cross over to her island. If she went the other way, she could die in the Everglades. Great. She had no idea what to do.

Hershel seemed to be attracted to the pathway to the left. It didn't seem to make as much sense to her, because she thought the right would take her to the coast- but then, she didn't really have a clue what direction she was in or where she was, so it was all just a guess based on the sun. But the paths could turn more down the way, and either one could head the right way eventually.

She decided to follow Hershel's lead.

They continued on.

Hours went by again, but still with no end of the path in sight.

We have to be lost, she thought. *There's no way this was the same way we came before.* But she had no choice but to see where it took her. At some point the path became merely just grass indents that seemed like other animals had created the trail. It was likely not the right one. But Hershel plodded along anyway. He seemed to think he knew what he was doing.

She sighed. *Well, at least when we die, I can blame it on the horse,* she laughed to herself. Maybe laughter was a sign of losing her mind. That made her laugh more. She was tired. She was hungry. And she was scared to do another night with all those creatures.

But they kept going and going. Marsh after bush after palm after marsh. The scenery all looked the same to her.

Until she saw what looked like smoke in the distance. Was there a camp ahead? Maybe a town?

She aimed Hershel down the side of the trees, leaving the path they were on but heading towards what she hoped was a better one.

The grass and tree line opened up to a wide pasture and she could see the smoke coming from just beyond.

Oh, but what if it is from some awful renegade soldiers or more scary white men… or even another band of Seminole? She stopped Hershel and leaned forward in her saddle to try to peer through the forest ahead of her. But she couldn't see anything.

She decided to walk him next to her instead of leaving him. He was her only way out of here except her own two feet, and she didn't want to lose him. If there were people nearby, they could try to steal her horse.

They walked through the woods and got to a point where she could finally make out the campfire ahead. It was burning next to some tents. She sighed, disappointed. She really wanted it to be a town; that there would be some people left who spoke English and could feed her and help her look at a map and figure out how to get home. But it wasn't a town.

She stood there, silently scoping out the situation. And then she saw something that caught her eye. It was a dog. A shepherd, that looked a lot like her own dog she'd left behind at the light station. She stared at it, as it ran around dragging a piece of wood in its mouth. It ran back to one of the tents and she heard a man's voice speak to it.

"Cyril, get it!" and the wood went flying across the grass. The dog bounded after it.

It wasn't Stormy, she realized. Her head drooped. She sure missed that dog. She hoped she was okay and that someone was feeding her while she was out here in the woods missing.

She looked up and she realized the man had seen her movement in the trees when the dog ran towards her direction. Oh, no. She didn't want to be seen yet. But she couldn't run. She had no other ideas of what to do or where to go.

"Is someone there?" the man called out. He walked towards her, and the dog trotted along by his side. She could see he was wearing a green coat and big, black boots. He was well dressed for a renegade soldier. Nothing he wore seemed to be from the military. She saw he held a rifle, but it was at his side. He wasn't expecting any danger, but Charlotte knew he should be. It was around them all of the time. Maybe he was the danger.

But she couldn't risk being lost in the woods forever. She had to reveal herself. Besides, he was good to his dog and didn't seem as dingy as the renegade men she'd met in the past.

"My name is Charlotte," she said, stepping into the clearing where the light could shine on her face. "I'm sorry to bother you. I saw your dog and it reminded me of my dog. And I'm lost…" Her voice trailed off, unsure what this man was doing here or what he wanted and not wanting to say too much.

"This is Cyril," he said, smiling. "I am Jacob. Why are you out here in this horrid place?"

She laughed. "It is quite horrid, isn't it?"

He nodded, still looking inquisitively at her.

She tried to tell him the story in a few sentences, but she stumbled on how awful the situation was. "I was working at the Cape Florida lighthouse. The Seminole captured me and took me to their camp. I got away but I need to get home…"

He walked quickly to her side and took Hershel's reins from her. "You are probably so hungry and tired. You need to rest. I have some food and I will take you to where there are other people who can help you. Being captured must have been a horrible and very scary adventure." He put his hand on her arm, "Let's get you somewhere safe."

She let him lead her to the tent and she sat down near his fire that was still burning brightly. He put Hershel with his horses. He had a few of them that she had not noticed beyond the tent. Then he came over to sit next to her. He motioned to some salted fish and a container full of water next to her, just beyond the fire.

She nodded, not too proud to accept the help at that point. She put the jug up to her mouth, guzzling the water. She had to slow herself down as she ate the fish so she wouldn't choke. Even if it was just some over-salted fish, at that moment it was the best food she had ever eaten. She had not eaten properly in days.

"Why are you here?" she asked him when she finally stopped chewing.

"I'm scouting the way for the rest of my group," he explained. "We are trying to get down to Key West. We heard it is safer down there and we need to check on our friends. After the hurricane we heard there were many deaths in the Keys, but nothing specific so we decided to go down to help and to find everyone if they survived."

She raised her head from where she had propped it on her knees and stared at him. "I'm also worried about people in Key West," she admitted. "It's been horrible not knowing what happened to them."

"It was an awful storm," Jacob agreed. "We must get down there as soon as possible." Then his eyebrows raised, and he looked her straight in the eyes. "You should actually just join us and go with us. Don't bother to go back to your station. It's not safe out here and our group has guns and enough food and supplies."

She shook her head. "No, I need to get back to the light station," she insisted. "John and Aaron…"

But he cut her off. "The light station is likely gone now." He saw her eyes drop. "I am so sorry your friends were there. But maybe they made it to safety too. Maybe they are on their way to Key West already."

She shrugged, "but what if they aren't?"

He kept going, "We heard a loud explosion from the island before we left Miami," he explained. "I think the Seminole burned it down. There was a lot of smoke, according to our friends who came from the direction and warned us to pack up and head out immediately after that."

Charlotte didn't want to hear that. She kept shaking her head. "No…. no…. no… John and Aaron were in the light tower, and they were going to light it for the night and then get out. They likely dove into the water below and got out of there. I think they will be okay. They have to be okay…."

She knew she must sound hysterical. But she couldn't accept that they were dead. SHE was the one missing, they couldn't be.

Jacob reached out one of his hands to touch hers. "I'm sorry, Charlotte. I am sure all of this is incredibly difficult for you. I hope they are okay too."

He offered her one of his blankets to lay on the ground next to them so she could spread out and avoid the thorny palm grass.

She moved her body as if in a trance, and sat where she could spread her legs out and rearrange her skirt and petticoat. She looked down at her ridiculous outfit that was all ripped and filthy, and her thoughts revolved around how awful it was. She sat there in her "proper" skirt that was soaked with sweat and probably full of ticks and spiders. And the two men that she was still dressing up for back at the light station, in what seemed like a whole other life, could now be gone. They could have burned up in that explosion. Jacob seemed to imply that they were likely killed. None of it was making sense and it seemed like such a comedy of errors.

Her gaze moved back to Jacob's face. She stared as if she could see right through him. "I have to find them if they are alive."

He agreed. "I think the best way to do that is to head to Key West and find your family and then return to look for them once you have more people." He ignored her shaking her head. "You can't possibly do it alone. I wouldn't even want to cross that waterway alone, especially because you will be seen for miles if you are in that water. The Seminole have been watching all crossings. They've left scouts at all sorts of points to watch for Americans. If you are caught again, I don't think you will be so lucky."

Charlotte knew he was right. And she was still torn over who to search for first. If she was heading south along this path by chance, she knew she was closer to Andrew; but if she was heading east, she knew she would hit the coast and could get back to the light station.

She had no idea what she would have done if she was heading west- that would have been sure death from being lost in the Everglades forever, probably.

And north would have likely taken her up to Fort Lauderdale where she could have found a way to the fort there and find people to help her. Whatever way she went other than west, she could still fulfill a purpose.

So, now she probably should focus on getting to Andrew. Jacob made it more than clear that was the best option, and he was probably right. She needed Andrew and whoever else would help her return to get John and Aaron. Even if they were dead and she just went to bury them…

She leaned back and relaxed against the blanket. "Okay," she said softly. "Okay." She had a plan.

Chapter Nineteen

Jacob took her through the woods the next day to meet the rest of his search party.

She had slept well, counting on him to keep an eye out for anything that could harm them. She dreamed of John and Aaron. John, with his big blue eyes staring into hers and telling her he needed her. And Aaron, with his soft brown eyes and gentle ways of letting her know she was cared for. Aaron put his hand on hers and she squeezed it in her dream, holding tightly to her best friend and all he stood for. She loved them both and missed them terribly. She woke with tears on her cheeks and with an even stronger will to get Andrew so she could go find them.

She and Jacob finished packing up and headed down the trail, Charlotte learned more about Jacob and his group.

He explained how he and a few other men had ventured ahead to scope for Seminole or other dangers. They were about a mile ahead of the rest of his family and friends who had left in a large herd of horses and people from the outskirts of the town of Miami. He said there were approximately thirty people total, with mostly men and a few women and children.

"And dogs," he said. "There are a lot of dogs left behind from the others who had already gone to Key West or headed north out of Florida. We gathered all of the dogs and threw them in a wagon," he laughed. "The wife and kids insisted we take them. I don't know what we will do with them, but we now are a traveling dog pack more than anything."

She laughed at the image. He said there were at least seven to ten dogs along with the group. That should help keep the coyotes at bay, she figured. And it would be nice to see more dogs. She enjoyed watching Cyril run next to Jacob's horse and dash back and forth along the trail, scaring the birds and squirrels on the way.

She hoped they could find Stormy when she returned to the light station. She hoped she could survive in the meanwhile. It was going to be a long time before she could get back there now. Probably a couple more weeks. That long wait would possibly kill her spirit if the elements and all the other dangers didn't. She sighed and followed Jacob and the three extra horses he was leading through the trees.

Jacob introduced her the other men when they met up with them a little later. He explained that they had all gone different directions in order to scope out the trail and circled around to get back together every other day and talk about what they had each witnessed.

It was working- they found some Seminoles a few days back, who were camping just beyond where they otherwise would have stumbled on them if they were in a larger group and not paying as much attention. They had avoided that area and skirted around the camp.

They had not seen any troops, they told her. Which was odd because the news that had originally been sent from the military to each town had guaranteed they would be patrolling the region and keeping the townspeople safe.

Charlotte realized it was a good idea that most of her town had evacuated. If they hadn't, more would have died when Natto and his group attacked the light station.

She shuddered just thinking about how much destruction the Natives caused, and how much more would have happened if there were more people involved. She wondered what other structures they had destroyed in town before getting to the lighthouse.

It was comforting being in a group of several men who all spoke English so she could understand what they were talking about, and who all had guns. What a shame the world had come to that- she would have rather hung out with Mica and her family in the old days, without English-speaking white men at all, and without guns. But now she had to fear her own best friend and her family. It seemed unreal and awful.

She listened to the men discuss the route and then Jacob offered to be the messenger for the rest of the party. He wanted to introduce Charlotte to the other women and have her ride with them so he could go back to scouting with the other men.

Charlotte agreed. She hadn't been very talkative with any of them, as she was lost in her thoughts and likely even in shock after the week's events. She would be more of a liability in the scouting group than any help right now.

Jacob guided her through the trees and eventually they came across the bigger group of wagons and horses. And all the dogs.

Jacob hadn't exaggerated- there were about ten dogs running about underfoot.

"Charlotte, this is Ada, my wife," Jacob said after leading her to one of the wagons that was stopped for everyone to walk around a little to stretch their legs. And for the dogs to drink some water. She saw a woman who was probably a few years older than she was, with a short skirt and short-sleeved blouse sitting next to the fire. She had a kind smile and a few wrinkles that hinted at a life of working outside instead of sitting in a life of luxury indoors. It was the mark of a frontier woman. Charlotte instantly knew she would like Ada.

"Hello Ada," Charlotte greeted her. "I appreciate Jacob finding me when I was lost in the woods. I am so glad to see friendly faces after so many days wandering and being stuck so deep in the Everglades."

"You poor thing," Ada gasped as she heard more details about Charlotte's adventures. They chatted for a while and Charlotte helped her gather some of the laundry she had hanging to dry around the wagon.

"We need to get you cleaned up. You are welcome to come along with us to Key West. We will find your brother there," Ada insisted after she had heard enough of the tale. "You don't need to help with these clothes. We need to get you something to wear yourself!"

Charlotte was grateful to have a chance to wash herself in the stream and Ada found her some new clothing to wear that mostly fit her, from her stack of items that were recently cleaned. "I will get new things in Key West," Ada smiled. "You need that clothing more than I do right now."

Charlotte added Hershel to the extra horses that were walking behind the wagons, and then she jumped up next to Ada in the front of the wagon. They were ready to get back on the trail.

Charlotte was pleased to see a woman driving a wagon and she relaxed, knowing this was a safe group to be with. As long as they could continue to avoid being attacked along the way, they could make it to Key West. According to Jacob, they were close to the coast and Charlotte had been on track when she was wandering to make it somewhere that she could have possibly crossed the bay and gone back to the island eventually, had she continued. So, Hershel was correct and was heading home after all. Which meant that she had not lost any ground and was now turning south with the wagon train.

Jacob's group was heading south along the coast, and they estimated it would take a couple more days to get to Key West. They would stop at Key Largo on the way, tomorrow, and stock up on any necessary supplies, and then head through the Marathon area where the hurricane had killed so many of the CCC workers who were there to build the new road. Jacob's friends assured her that there was now a way through, as a temporary route was made along the old road area. But it would be hard for her to stomach all that damage. The idea of seeing so much evidence of so many lives lost was making her ill long before they ever reached that area. From what the men read from the papers they were finally getting access to along the route, there were no trees down there, and much of the island of Marathon was still under water.

It would be a difficult day. But it could be even harder the following day when they made it to Key West, if they were able to keep up that kind of pace. No one knew what to expect in Key West.

They kept going and going. The day was long and hot and humid and the kids and dogs eventually tired of running next to the wagons and piled in behind them and fell asleep.

Eventually they stopped for a late dinner and made a fire. Charlotte was nervous that the Seminole might see the smoke, but the scouts had ridden pretty far ahead and out to the sides of where they stopped for the evening, and they said there were no people to be seen for miles. They were in the area next to the thickest part of the swamps. It was a shallow, grassy river for miles and miles in every direction around them except for to the east where the Atlantic Ocean flanked the land.

Charlotte looked forward to seeing the white beaches and aqua waters of the Keys. She always heard they were beautiful. She hoped the hurricane had not ruined the islands so much that they could not see those views she imagined. It would sure beat seeing the Everglades for a while.

She concentrated on the hope of seeing those tropical views instead of thinking hard about all of the potential scary things they might see instead.

She was definitely ready to get to some towns and

to go inside a real building and to be surrounded by more people… to see stores… to take a real bath…

It was definitely time to search for Andrew and Catharine and the kids. She hoped more than anything that she would be able to find them and that they were okay.

Chapter Twenty

Finding Andrew and Catharine proved to be anything but easy. It seemed like going to a little island and asking around for someone would be simple enough, but Charlotte had not realized first of all, how many islands they had to go through in order to even get to Key West.

Then, she had not realized the devastation from what they were told now was an actual hurricane, that they would have to traverse to get there. She also could not have predicted the number of people who had flooded into the keys in order to assist with the rebuilding efforts… and those who were there to make a quick buck by taking advantage of those in the middle of the chaos.

Jacob and Ada were gracious hosts, allowing Charlotte to earn her keep by tending to the dogs, horses, and occasionally the children. She didn't mind the monotony of feeding animals and she spent as much time as possible hugging their furry little bodies. She wondered what happened to Stormy and hoped she had made it somewhere safe and was finding food. Thankfully she still had Hershel to keep her company. He was the constant familiar face she could count on, even if he was much more concerned about the grain that she doled out from the bag on the supply wagon than her actual personality.

The first few days of travel on the road through the Keys were not as difficult as she thought they would be. The townsfolk from Miami and the smaller homesteads along the way had quickly traversed that route to try to reach the civilization on Key Largo. They already had cleared the downed palms and shoveled tons and tons of sand so they could rebuild the road and repair some of the broken railway.

Charlotte and Jacob's party camped along the narrow beaches near the new roadways, sometimes having to clear debris from the ground to even have an area to park the wagons and corral the horses.

By the fourth day, the travelers were having to walk the horses and wagons over rickety boards and marshy areas where the sea had broken through the island and created streams where the road used to be.

Charlotte was tired and hot and dirty. The saltwater beaches were beautiful, but salt water was not the best for washing skin, and the dry salt chapped her legs. They found some fresh water streams a couple of times and it felt amazing to wash off the salt and sand that was caked all over her body, especially in all the areas that rubbed together when walking.

The hat Ada loaned her to wear was helping keep sun off the top of her head, but as the sun rose and sank it hit her cheeks and nose anyway.

She had never traveled like this in the Florida heat in the past. When her family moved to the lighthouse when she was younger, she remembered lots of short travel days and stops at towns along the way where she could clean up and eat cooked food and so forth. This kind of travel, watching out for Indian attacks and having to actually trailblaze and rush towards the Keys was not the same at all.

She longed for the security of an actual building, rather than sleeping in the wagon or in tents along the temporary dirt roads and chaos as people rushed back and forth along the route. She longed for her family.

Being so close to Andrew and yet so far was tearing her up. She had a headache for days and she wasn't sure if it was the heat or the dehydration from long days on the roads, or the noise from the busy towns and wagons, or if it was just that worrying about what she might find was overwhelming her mind.

She continued to do what was needed each day. She rose with the sun and slept hard when it finally went down and gave them a small break from its rays. She fed the animals and chased the children and helped with the meals. She talked to everyone along the road who had a moment to share information, and she ate up every bit of news that Jacob and his friends shared with her from their scouting missions ahead of the main group. The news was sometimes grim, and sometimes hopeful. She smiled politely and hugged the others when they received good news about their family members.

Tara and Joseph, an older couple who was traveling with some of the other younger families in the back of the wagon train were excited to hear that their son was accounted for and that he had sent word of his location so they could see each other when the group reached

Key West.

Charlotte was eager to see that reunion and genuinely thrilled for their excitement and relief. But it reminded her again of how much she didn't know about her own loved ones. What if Andrew and Catharine and the kids were not okay? What if she hoped for such a reunion and counted on it, and then had devastating news instead? She wouldn't let herself think much about it, even though her whole body was tense with that worry hanging over her days.

And then they finally reached Key West.

It was about ten times as busy as the other island towns had been. As they crossed the bridge and made their way through the streets, she was pleased to see that although the roads were missing rocks in many places, it wasn't as terrible as in the middle Keys. There were some areas that had been redone, likely due from the waters rising and tearing them up. The trees and bushes were thin, likely from high winds ripping them apart. But the old buildings had weathered the storm much better than she had expected. They were built with solid wood frames and many in the downtown area were linked together along the town blocks, so they must have been strong enough to make it. Plus, from what she was hearing, the storm was a little less intense in Key West than in Marathon where the eye went through. Which meant they had a lot of people still there and it was a busy hub of economic activity.

The problem was getting everything down there, so they were still waiting for several types of supplies, like big beams and lumber to repair some of the structures that needed fixing, and a lot of the food staples were running low. The marina was busy with ships coming and going and Charlotte noticed the light station on the island was busy at work. That made her wonder about her own light, up in Key Biscayne, and her friends she had abandoned there.

"Hey, watch where you're going!" a man yelled at her, as she missed a step and almost fell in his path as he rode by on a bicycle.

Those thoughts and the accompanying guilt would kill her if she didn't get back up to the lighthouse soon. And in order to do that, she needed Andrew and whoever else could accompany them, so she wouldn't have to do it all alone this time.

She stared at the receding bicyclist and hoisted her skirt up higher so she could step into the store entrance. Ada asked her to grab some goods for her family who was staying with cousins at a small residence nearby. Charlotte felt more than lucky to have met such nice people, as they included her in their family situation, even while knowing they didn't have to do so.

"Good morning, Ma'am," the storekeeper greeted her as she entered. "Can I help you find anything specific?"

Charlotte looked around the room, seeing some of the items on her list already. "Thank you. I think I will be able to find what we need," she said. "I am shopping for the Wilkerson family who say they have an account with you. I hope that is the case."

She moved towards the vegetable counter and went to grab a few tomatoes, when she looked up at the storekeeper to smile his way and await his response.

"Yes, we have an account for the Wilkersons," he was saying.

She heard his words but was frozen in place, staring at him in awe.

"Asa?" she gasped. She recognized his dark hair and chiseled face and realized this was one of the men who had stayed at the keepers' house with her family before they traveled south to the Keys.

She watched his eyes widen too, as he ran towards her, "Charlotte?" he cried out, "Charlotte DuBose?"

She let him hug her and they danced around in excitement. If Asa made it, surely Andrew and his family did too. She felt the hope rise inside of her.

"Asa, I am so glad to see you," she said, pulling back to look at him. "I just made it down here last night. I am here to find my brother's family. Have you seen Andrew?"

"Oh, Charlotte, I am so happy you are okay and you made it out of that area. I've heard so many things. We thought you'd perished when the lighthouse was burned down. The soldiers from the ships that stopped by the island and saw the damage came down here with terrible news."

She nodded, her mind flashing back on that terrible morning when she watched the lighthouse flames above the keepers' cabin roof. The last time she ever saw her home… and Aaron, and John…

"But… what about Andrew?" she asked, pleading with her eyes for some news.

"Andrew and Catharine are okay. The kids are fine too," he said, nodding and hugging her again as she threw herself towards him at such amazing information.

"Oh, thank you! Thank you!" she cried out. "Where are they? I need to see them."

"They live near the marina and assist with the map planning and assorted other jobs that help those who sail the waterways around here. I can have someone take you there," he offered.

Charlotte was beside herself with relief and excitement. To see them would be one less thing to worry about and would surely help her get one step closer to returning to the light station and finding Aaron and John.

Asa had her wait while he went to the back of the building and came back with one of his teenaged sons. "Chris will help take you to Andrew and Catharine's residence," he said, helping her bag up the few things Ada needed. "I will mark this on your friends' account and send the items over to their house now, so you can get right to seeing your family."

She thanked him profusely as she rushed out the door with Chris, who was a gangly teen with fast legs and a big smile.

"I am so thankful for you for taking the time to make sure I find my family," Charlotte told Chris as they made their way through alleyways and down towards the water.

He smiled and nodded and they hurried on their way.

Key West indeed was beautiful. It seemed much more beautiful in the light than Charlotte had seen when first arriving late the night before. And now, knowing that Andrew was okay, and she was on her way to see his family made everything shine with a new glow. She ran next to Chris, aware that he was in just as much of a hurry to get her there so he could get back to whatever he had been doing as she was to see her family. Which was fine with her. She just wanted to get there right away.

They made it to the front door, where Chris knocked loudly on the old wood and called out, "Mr. DuBose?"

They heard footsteps and then the door was pulled open, and a white and somewhat elderly woman Charlotte had never seen before stuck her head out. "Can

I help you?"

"Hello," Charlotte said, stepping in front of Chris. "I am looking for my brother, Andrew DuBose or his wife, Catharine DuBose."

The woman's eyes widened, and she pulled Charlotte by the arm into the coolness of the front room. Charlotte waved to Chris, and he laughed at the eager woman dragging Charlotte inside the house.

"Oh my," the older woman said, "you must be the missing Charlotte!" She hugged Charlotte to her thick bosom and almost pushed her into the chair near the door. "You just sit here, and I will get you something to drink while we wait for them. They will be more than excited to see you. They have been so worried about you. Everyone thought you'd been killed!"

Charlotte's head was spinning from the quick actions of this woman and from the change in brightness from the outside sun to the dark indoor lighting. She looked towards the door and saw Chris' backside wandering down the road, already on his way back to the store.

So, this was where her family ended up, Charlotte thought. They made it.

She sighed with relief. This was better than she could have hoped for. She looked around the living area beyond her chair and saw it was sparsely furnished. She saw some family photographs along the walls and recognized some of the little things they had brought with them to make a new home here.

"Charlotte?" she heard a little voice in the hallway just beyond. She looked towards the familiar sound and saw her sweet niece, Margaret standing there, looking just as shocked as the woman who was now making noise in the kitchen as she poured something for Charlotte to drink.

"Margaret!" Charlotte cried out. She jumped up and ran across the room to embrace the small child.

"Oh, Aunt Charlotte," Margaret cried, "we have missed you so much."

She looked over Margaret's little head and saw an even smaller body entering the room. "Fred!" she called to him, letting him also join her and Margaret as they all hugged each other and cried happy tears.

She kept looking back and forth between her niece and nephew, so thankful to see them doing so well. They were smiling and jumping around the room, showing her everything and telling her stories about the journey down there and all the fun they have been having in the new town.

"Where are your parents?" Charlotte finally got a word in and asked them as they all settled down. The children were still hanging on her skirt, refusing to let go as if they were worried that this was all just a strange and wonderful dream.

"We don't really know," Margaret said. "I woke early this morning to some loud voices, and someone was saying something about the hospital. I'm worried, but no one will tell us anything."

Charlotte felt her breath stop for a moment. The hospital? What could have happened? Did she come all this way to find her brother and now he was ill or hurt? She needed to find him right away.

The woman who had opened the door returned to the room, "here is some lemonade for you, Ms. Charlotte," she said. "I see you've found the children," she smiled kindly towards the three of them, still huddled together.

"I did," Charlotte smiled through her stress. "But I heard there was something about a hospital this morning and I really do need to get to Andrew and Catharine," she pleaded.

"Yeah, Miss Angel," the kids pleaded, "can you help us find Mom and Dad?"

"Oh, they are okay, Charlotte," the woman who Charlotte figured was Miss Angel," stated. "They just went to help with someone else who was injured. They will be back soon, I'm sure."

Charlotte sighed, "I'm glad to hear they are okay. I was certainly worried. But I must see them as soon as possible. We had friends at the light station who I left behind. I need to find them and make sure they are okay."

Miss Angel nodded and put her hand on her shoulder, "Charlotte, you need to take a breath. Take some time to finish your drink and we can wait for them to return."

Charlotte took a drink of the sweet concoction and smiled politely. "I appreciate this, Miss Angel," she said. "I will indeed finish this lovely drink. But then I must go directly to the hospital."

The kids hugged her tighter, afraid to let go.

"I will come back and spend time with you, I promise," Charlotte told them. "I just need to see your parents and talk to them right away."

She pulled herself from their arms and kissed them both on their heads. "I am so glad you all are doing well down here. I was so worried about you after the storm."

"It was so windy," Margaret said, nodding.

"We thought we would die from the waves coming through the streets," Fred added. "But we were okay. We stayed upstairs until the water went back down."

"We were certainly lucky," Miss Angel agreed.

"I'm so glad to hear this," Charlotte said, hugging the kids one more time. "I will be back," she said, letting Miss Angel take the glass from her hands and help her open the door.

Miss Angel nodded. "Do you know where the hospital is?" she asked.

Charlotte shook her head. "I will ask someone to take me," she admitted.

"You can find it just down the way. They have a triage center set up just beyond the docks, at the edge of town. About five blocks. You should be able to walk it."

Charlotte thanked her and hurried outside. "I will find them and hopefully return when they do."

Miss Angel nodded and wished her well.

Charlotte was thankful for the shade on this side of the street as she meandered through the passing pedestrians and horses and made her way to where Miss Angel had directed. The sunshine was hot down there in Key West, but she was just happy to be on this journey as it was beyond time for her to find her brother. She couldn't wait to give him the largest hug ever.

Chapter Twenty-One

The lady at the front desk led Charlotte down the humid walkway towards the room where she said Andrew and Catharine would be, she could feel herself building up with anticipation. It would be so amazing to see them. It was beyond incredible knowing that they were okay and thriving down here in the Keys. But seeing them in person would make it all seem more real.

She rounded the hallway and started to enter the door that the receptionist pointed to. But just as she was rushing forward a guy stepped in front of her and stopped her by putting his hand in front of her before she could even get her foot across the threshold.

"I'm sorry, you can't enter," the man dressed in white and a matching white face mask told her sternly.

"I have to enter. My brother and sister-in-law are in there and I just came from very far away to find them," she begged.

He shook his head. "You can't go in there. No one else can go in there," he said.

She saw a nametag on his shirt, signifying that he was a nurse and worked at the Key West hospital.

Her shoulders weakened and drooped. She could feel tears rushing to her eyes. "Can I wait here? Can you tell Andrew that I am out here?"

He shrugged. Then he went back into the room.

There was a loud commotion inside and then she was being dragged back from the door by the force of the man who rushed out of the room and grabbed her. "Charlotte?!" she recognized the wiry hair and giant eyes of the man who was now rocking her in his arms like a big baby.

"Andrew!" She gasped. "Andrew!" she didn't even know what to say. She hugged him back, the two of them almost falling to the floor before he balanced them by grabbing a chair next to the entrance.

"I thought you were dead," he cried. She had never seen such big tears rolling down his face before. "I thought you were gone, and I was so devastated by the news of the loss of the light station because I figured you were all dead."

She was also crying tears of joy and relief. "I am obviously not dead, Andrew," she smiled through the tears, "as you can see."

He nodded, holding her to him all over again. She looked over his shoulder and saw Catharine rushing out of the room just beyond the one Andrew had come from.

"I heard your voice," Catharine cried out. "I thought it must be a ghost!" she joined them in a huge hug.

When they finally were able to catch their breaths and had exhausted themselves from dancing and hugging over and over again, Andrew asked about Aaron. "What about Aaron? Did he make it out, too?" he asked. "Is he okay?" He looked around like he expected Aaron to pop his head in the room any time.

She could see him holding his breath. Charlotte noticed he hadn't mentioned John, but then she realized he may not even know yet that he had stayed too.

She shook her head, "I don't know how they are, or how the light station is," she admitted. "Mica's family took me, and I didn't see what happened. I would have otherwise been more helpful. I feel terrible to have left," she said. Then the reality of the situation hit her. She was there, but they were not. She felt her tears fall from her eyes for the first time in what seemed like forever. She felt safe enough to finally let down her guard. But she'd failed to save their friends and didn't even know enough to give Andrew and Catharine any news.

"Oh, Charlotte," Catharine gasped. "That must have been so scary."

She nodded, "there were times when it was. But I was trying to distract the Seminole for long enough for them to get to safety," she explained. "There were so many of them and we were surrounded."

"You did not let anyone down," Andrew said. "No one else was willing to stay behind like you and Aaron were."

Charlotte almost was about to explain that John was there too, when Andrew stopped her.

"Wait, who else was with you?" Andrew asked, finally catching on to her reference to her trying to help more than one person at the light. "You keep saying 'we'…"

Charlotte nodded. "John Thompson stayed behind to help us too."

Andrew's eyes widened. "Oh, wow…" he said, "I

was sure he had just gone with another group and was with his sister's family or something." She could see the breath essentially knocked out of him as he realized what it meant that Charlotte was here, and Aaron and John were not. And that there were two men missing, not just one.

"I tried to help them," she whispered, hanging her head.

Andrew's face changed from a look of pure devastation to one of anger at all that had happened to his family, their friends, and their light station.

After a few minutes of silence he said, "We will have to talk more soon. But let's get you safe and comfortable at home."

"Well, are you done with what you were doing here?" she asked, motioning back to the door of the room he had been in. "Does someone else need you? Because I can wait…" She imagined with all of the commotion going on around them, the hospital staff and all the other people who were being treated there needed more help than she did.

"I can't do more for anyone right now," he said. "We just have to wait and see if these men will recover.

We've done what we could do."

Charlotte wasn't sure what they were up to behind those walls, but she knew it must be serious.

Catharine must have noticed Charlotte's expression. She explained, "Andrew has been helping the doctors with medical assistance since there just aren't enough people to help with all the injuries from the war."

Charlotte took a deep breath. It was impressive how much the two of them had stepped in to help the community in Key West. "They are so lucky to have your help. It seems that it was a good idea that you all came down here," she said. "Much safer here too."

They both nodded, while grabbing their supplies and getting ready to go home with her.

She hung her head, "I'm sorry I was unable to hold down the fort at the light station better."

"Stop, Charlotte," Andrew said, patting her hand. "Let's go home."

They all walked down the hall together, holding each other, with their footsteps the only noise. There was not much more to be said at that moment.

Chapter Twenty-Two

It didn't take much to convince Andrew to agree to go back to the light station with Charlotte.

He nodded enthusiastically when she mentioned it.

"I've been telling Catharine for weeks that I needed to go back to get you, like I promised," he said. "It just got so busy here and it was harder to go back after the storm than any of us anticipated. The roads were ruined and people were hurt. The ones who were shipped down here from hurricane injuries filled up the hospital but then they kept bringing war victims in too… They just needed so much help."

"I know," she said. "I figured you would try to get back to me if you could. I was sure worried about you all when the storm blew through. I could tell it was a huge one."

"We were without any supplies or any link to the

rest of the world for a while."

Charlotte imagined how hard it must have been. But at least the city of Key West was not as damaged as what happened in Marathon.

"I think before we get ready to go back up north, we should go talk to some of my friends here," Andrew suggested. "I know some people who know some people, if you know what I mean. Powerful people. Men who are running some major businesses out of this little place."

Charlotte's eyes widened. "That would be amazing if other people could help too," she agreed.

"One of my friends, Rich Fitzgerald runs a wrecking company. He and his people go out and take apart shipwrecks. They've made a lot of money doing it, too. They have boats and they have the ability to take us along the coast instead of having to go the interior route where the Seminole continue to attack."

She nodded, "That's a great idea." She knew sitting on a boat in the waves could be another kind of horror if she got seasick like many people do, but risking another attack by the Natives sounded horrible. The things nightmares are made of. And she had enough of those to last quite a while.

They decided she would meet Mr. Fitzgerald as soon as possible and then they would concoct a more complete plan when they were able to get his input.

It took a day to schedule an appointment with Mr. Fitzgerald. He was apparently much busier than Charlotte imagined, even if he was on an island with only five hundred or so people. He ran such a successful operation that everyone in town needed to talk to him about something, it seemed.

When she finally did meet him, she could see why. He was a loud and commanding person who lit up the room with his big laugh and charming personality. But he was rough, like the kind of man who you imagined working directly with pirates, which is of course what those who did not like his business accused him of doing. Someone tough enough to be willing to help them return in the middle of the Indian War was just what they needed.

"Well, hello, Miss Charlotte," he bellowed, leaning in for a proper handshake and she felt compelled to even courtesy a little, which was unlike her. But he was one of the kinds of men who she could tell you needed to play up to if you wanted to get anything done with their support.

"I'm pleased to meet you," she smiled. "I hear you might be able to help us get back home to check on our light station in Key Biscayne. I've been told that if anyone could get us back there, you would be the one to talk to."

He stared at her, laughing at her blunt request. "Is that so?" he grinned, looking over her shoulder to Andrew, who was trying to move up next to her before she excluded him from the discussion altogether.

"I'm sorry, Rich," Andrew laughed nervously. "Charlotte is known for her ability to get things done too, like you… And apparently she believed all the wonderful things I said about you and your abilities."

The men shook hands and Mr. Fitzgerald got right down to business.

"I have a ship returning from around the Key Biscayne area today or tomorrow. They've been salvaging vessels off the coast there and sent a message with another ship that they were on their way back a couple days ago. So, it should be anytime. I can let you know what we hear from them when they return. Then we could book you passage with them on their way back out again, after they restock and change some crew."

"That would be amazing," Charlotte said, looking to Andrew for agreement.

He was not as quick to respond, taking a minute to chew on the idea. "I think we could be ready to go within a couple of days," he finally said. "But what will this cost us?"

Charlotte did not have any money at that point. She had not even thought about money in weeks, or even months it seemed. Everything on this journey had been paid for by her work and efforts to jump in and be useful on the wagon train with Jacob and Ada. Even the account with Asa at the general store was based on a trade system. But she knew how unrealistic it was to believe she could just get free passage on a ship to take her over a hundred nautical miles somewhere; especially somewhere dangerous.

She sighed, feeling defeated. She had no idea what she could possibly do for that kind of money. Perhaps she could get a job in town and work for a while until she had enough. But if that was the case, she would waste so much time getting back to the light station that she might as well brave the journey by horseback again. If they could even find their way without trouble. With all the towns deserted up there and the Keys railroad and roads all under construction, it could take just as long to get back. Especially if they were surprised by the Seminole on the way.

Mr. Fitzgerald shrugged. "My boat is going back there even if you don't ride along," he said. "I imagine there will be food costs, and additional work for the crew, but I think we could figure something out."

Andrew visibly relaxed, his shoulders dropping slightly and his chin raising. "My friend," he said, "I owe you so much for this kind of help."

"Think nothing of it," Mr. Fitzgerald smiled again. "I will need some additional charts created though, with the new information about the wrecks that they found along the way. Perhaps you can help us with those?"

Andrew nodded and they shook on it. "I will prepare whatever you need along the way."

"Let's first see what the crew has to say about what they saw up there before you decide how you want to proceed. Then we can schedule the departure more clearly if you still want to go."

They all agreed to meet up whenever the ship returned to the dock to the left of the schooner that was already floating outside their office building. Andrew figured he was always down at the docks working anyway, and he would put the word out for everyone he talked with to keep him posted in case the ship returned and he was not aware.

They returned home and discussed the plans with Catharine. She would stay behind with the children and Miss Angel, while Charlotte and Andrew headed up there by ship. Catharine was much more comfortable with the water approach than having them go by horseback, so it seemed as though the plan was coming together well.

Just as Mr. Fitzgerald predicted, the large ship returned that evening. Andrew was outside the house when one of his friends rode by on a horse, calling out to him, "the ship's back!"

Andrew found Charlotte who was inside helping Catharine and Margaret make some supper. "Let's go back to meet with Rich now," he said, grabbing his hat and motioning to the door. "The ship's here."

Charlotte apologized to Catharine for having to drop everything and run, but she understood. "Just try to be back soon. Dinner will be ready by then."

They agreed and were quickly out the door and rushing down the block.

"Oh, you heard the ship came in," Mr. Fitzgerald said as they walked around the building to where he stood, directing the removal of some large chests of what Charlotte figured were packed full of salvaged goods and other supplies. "I was just talking to the ship's master about sitting down to talk with you. I'm glad you're here."

He led them back into the cooler air of the building and they waited as he called to some of the men to join them.

"This is Pete, our ship's master and the master of many of our salvage operations," he said, pointing at a man with a deep tan from what Charlotte assumed must be days and days on boats in the sun. They nodded at each other.

"And this is Joe," he said. A thin man with what

seemed like a very quiet demeanor nodded their way too.

"My friends would like to hear about their light station at Key Biscayne. Mr. DuBose was the lighthouse keeper there and they are concerned with the welfare of their friends they left behind." Mr. Fitzgerald obviously didn't want to spare the time to tell the entire story they'd shared with him earlier, which was fine with Charlotte. The less emotional this discussion was, the better. She just wanted to know what these men knew, which was hard enough to think about.

"Well," Pete began slowly, "I don't think there's much of a light station left on Cape Florida now."

Charlotte nodded, "that's what we've been told."

"But it's possible that your friends could still be there. I have no idea. We were not close enough to the island to actually see what happened. We just heard the stories about the Seminole burning it down, and we didn't see no light out there."

"We had nothin' to do with extinguishing that light, though," Joe said, looking a bit stressed.

"Of course, we didn't," Pete said, knocking Joe in the arm with his fist. "That's punishable by death now a'days," he stated. "We ain't messin' with those light houses."

Andrew assured them they knew it was the Seminole who did it. There was no doubt after hearing Charlotte's version of the event, even from her weak vantage point, that it was that band of Natives who caused the problems at the light station that day, not wreckers.

Charlotte hung her head, trying not to sob out loud. If John or Aaron were still there, they would have found a way to light a light at some point. Maybe they were afraid the Seminole would return. But eventually, they still would want to signal that they were okay, wouldn't they? She didn't want to think about the alternate possibilities.

"The DuBoses would like a ride back up there," Mr. Fitzgerald said.

Joe and Pete both nodded. "It's a long haul since we go around a few wrecks and have a few things we need to do on the way. But we would be happy to have ya aboard," Pete said.

Mr. Fitzgerald explained that Andrew would be along to help with charting on the way. Joe perked up, telling them about some of the shipwrecks they were going to return to. "There's a lot of stuff on those ships along Carysfort," he said. "We took what we could on our first load but there's plenty left to finish unloading. Some don't seem to have been raided by pirates yet, so we have a chance to bring a lot of stuff back. You'll get to see some interesting things on our ship."

"We try to salvage things for the ships' owners," Joe stated, looking sideways at Pete for sounding like they were pirates themselves. "We unload ships that are stuck on the shoals, and we get rewards for helping save the cargoes by lightening the loads and then the ships can sometimes get off the rocks and be reloaded."

Charlotte was somewhat interested in what they were talking about doing, but mostly just wanted to hurry up and get back to the light station. Having to go around the wrecks would be annoying more than enjoyable at this point. But she was thankful for the opportunity to ride along if it meant getting there eventually.

They finalized plans to leave in three days. Charlotte wanted to go immediately, so three days sounded like forever to her. But they had to restock the ship and change out the crew like Mr. Fitzgerald warned would happen. Plus, there was a little storm brewing that they wanted to let pass first.

"It's no fun on the water when it's stormy," Pete assured them. "We will get back out there as soon as that passes."

They all went their separate ways.

Charlotte took another look at the ship from the window of the building. It was a rugged vessel, but it looked strong and capable of getting them where they needed to go. She noticed it had a sign on the back of the ship that said, "Elect Richard Fitzgerald to City Council."

She pointed it out to Andrew as they departed.

"Yeah, Rich has been on the Council multiple times. I guess when you have as much money as he has from all those wrecks, you can do whatever you want around here."

"He's a good person to know," Charlotte said. "Thank you for finding him for us. I can't wait to get on that ship and head up to the light station."

"Me too," he said, patting her arm.

She grabbed his hand and held onto it for a minute. "I sure am glad you're okay, Andrew," she said.

"I sure am glad you are, too."

They returned to the DuBose house to start the countdown to departure.

Chapter Twenty-Three

The storm came through town as predicted. Charlotte felt the first drops of rain and the gusty wind rattling the windows of the DuBose house and got chills. She knew this wasn't predicted to be as bad as the unnamed hurricane that wiped out the central Keys. But she still worried.

The family hunkered down inside and enjoyed knowing they were all together this time, even though Charlotte couldn't shake thoughts of Aaron and John out of her mind. She hoped they were somewhere safe this time too, and that they would be waiting for them when they returned to the station later that week.

She wondered about her dog, Stormy, and hoped somehow, that she had found her way back to Aaron and John and was safe too.

Charlotte visited Ada and Jacob a few times since

they'd all settled in Key West, and she always enjoyed seeing all the dogs they still were caring for. It reminded her of how comforting it was to have her own dog and she felt that familiar pulling at her heart.

Sometimes she lost herself in memories of John... John smiling at her... John laughing... John holding her in his arms. She remembered the way he smelled, like musky leather and soap, and the way he pushed her against the wall and trapped her so she had to give into his body, leaning into hers so she could feel every inch of him. She yearned for that contact. She'd lost track of time with all the travel and time spent finding her way to her family. But she figured it was going on a month since she'd last seen John and Aaron.

She wondered what Aaron was doing now without her there. He must be overcome with worry about her. He always was the one she could count on to find a way to make things better. And yet, nothing was going to be better until she knew he was okay.

The storm passed by almost as quickly as it came, and the family slept well.

In the morning, Charlotte woke to lots of loud

voices yelling in the street.

Soon someone knocked loudly at their door, calling to Andrew to come down to the docks.

"Hurry," they cried, "there's…" but Charlotte didn't hear the rest of what they said.

She put her dress on hastily and pulled her hair into a bun on her neck. Then she ran downstairs to see what was going on.

"There's a huge load of people coming in on ships at the dock," Catharine started filling her in. "There was a wreck off the coast of Tavernier and there were hundreds of people on board."

"Oh no," Charlotte gasped. "Are there survivors?"

"From what it sounds like, they rescued them all!" Catharine replied.

Charlotte didn't waste any time rushing out the door after Andrew, knowing they may need additional hands with so many people flooding into town. There may be injuries if the ship was wrecked. Also, with only several hundred people in the entire Key West city, she knew that everyone who could help would be appreciated and she appreciated all the help they'd given her family.

She was correct that all the volunteers were very appreciated. As soon as she arrived, they started calling orders to her, presuming she was there to assist.

"Start getting a list of all the people's names and where they are from. We need to know who we are dealing with," she was told.

Someone had created a makeshift waiting area and they were funneling everyone off the boats that were coming into the harbor into that part of the shipyard.

Charlotte walked from family to family collecting information. Some did not speak English well, and some had injuries that were being triaged by hospital staff and many of the women from town.

She watched as several men rushed onto the ship with a gurney to pick up the more severely injured.

People rushed about the area, collecting the people who had already checked in with Charlotte and rushing them into the street to be led by other volunteers to homes where they could clean up and rest. Anyone with extra space in their residences were taking in the strangers from the shipwrecked boat.

"I've never seen such a coordinated effort and such charity," Mr. Fitzgerald said loudly, as he directed people from the balcony of his building that was now the central point for all volunteers to check in and hear updates on what was happening. "I thank all of you, the residents of Key West, for such a quick and seamless operation."

Everyone was exhausted, and the town was bursting at its seams with extra people who needed much more than what the town usually could offer. But everyone picked up the slack.

Asa Tift brought out all of the extra supplies in his general store and had his son Chris helping keep a running log of who was using what items like extra clothing and food and cloth for bedding. He told them not to worry about the money yet.

Tents were set up in the shipyard and throughout the center of town for the remaining families who did not have available beds in the town's homes. More and more people were coming off more and more boats. Everyone who had a boat had gone out to help with the recovery and they kept coming back with more victims of the wreck.

Every spare hand was sent down to the hospital to help with the injured. However, there were surprisingly less injuries than one would have expected with such a large disaster.

Charlotte was surprised to see there were animals coming off the ships too. Some of the families had taken their pets with them on their journey to safety and even the dogs and cats were rescued along the shoals. This was probably one of the most amazing instances of a large ship actually staying afloat long enough for everyone to get unloaded that Charlotte had ever heard of. She was so glad to see the pets running around town with their families, and assorted packs of dogs that she knew would be sorted out and returned to their families. Active animals meant likely healthy and uninjured animals, so that made her feel like things were really going to be okay.

Until she noticed one of the dogs running through the streets… it was surprisingly like her Stormy. The same thick build and similar colors. But this one was a bit more dingy, like it had a rougher life than many of the others.

"Does anyone know whose dogs those are?" Charlotte pointed to the pack of about four dogs running past the hospital. But none of the people near her answered. Likely no one knew whose dogs they were, yet.

The shepherd dog was not staying with the others, it heard her voice and turned to look at her.

It couldn't possibly be her Stormy… Charlotte shook her head. But why was it staring at her like that? And why did it look so much like Stormy?

She patted her leg like she used to do for Stormy. The dog cocked its head and stared more.

She felt foolish even thinking it could be her dog. But it sure looked like Stormy. And why wasn't it running off?

She patted her leg again.

The dog slowly started walking her way.

Charlotte felt tears gathering in her eyes. If it wasn't Stormy, it sure was acting similar.

It seemed like a dream to see that dog react the way it was reacting towards her. Maybe she was imagining all of this.

But then she patted her leg one more time and the dog ran right up to her.

"Stormy?" she said, petting the dog's head, and the dog started licking her hands.

"Oh, my goodness," she wept. "Stormy!"

She didn't care who saw her now. This had to be her dog. It just had to be. No other dog would react this way. And it looked just like Stormy. Except she was so bony and seemed a little sickly too.

She hoped the dog would wait for her if she went inside and got a rope. She rushed into the hospital and asked if anyone had anything she could use to restrain a dog. They found her a twine rope that had come off one of their supply crates. "Will this work?"

She thanked the kind man who handed it to her and rushed back outside. Sure enough, the dog was still there.

She had no doubt in her mind anymore. This was her dog. But how could Stormy get all the way to Key West? Perhaps it came off the boats that were flooding the harbor with all the shipwreck victims. Maybe someone found her along Cape Florida on one of their journeys.

However it happened, she was just thankful to have her dog back. She tied the rope around her neck for a leash and led her back to Andrew's house. She had some explaining to do, and really had no idea what to tell him.

Except that her dog was back with her, and she was so thankful.

Charlotte asked Miss Angel and the kids to keep track of Stormy while she returned to check on what else was needed. Catharine had headed to the hospital earlier, so Miss Angel suggested she head back over there too.

She walked into the front reception space in the building and was overwhelmed by how many people were roaming around. At first, she thought they were all injured people. But after a while she realized that many were volunteers like herself, and a few were family members of those who were indeed hurt and receiving care.

She recognized the nurse who had kicked her out of the room when she was trying to find Andrew. He was busy scribbling notes on a pad of paper and running between rooms.

She saw Catharine standing in a doorway staring like she'd seen a ghost.

She ran over to her.

"What's wrong, Catharine?" Charlotte asked.

"Oh, Charlotte…" Catharine choked. "You have to

come with me."

Then she turned and walked back towards the back hallway of the hospital. Charlotte followed, wondering what kind of injuries had Catharine so upset. She had no clue what was waiting for her down the hall.

Chapter Twenty-Four

When Charlotte first entered the room that Catharine motioned for her to go inside, she had to adjust her eyes to the darkness.

She saw what seemed to be a doctor looking at some equipment, but he exited the room when she entered. Everyone cleared out of the room at that point. But Charlotte was too focused on what she saw ahead of her for her to even notice anyone else.

It was the sole wincey shirt on the chair next to the bed that first made her gasp. The same khaki color with the patch on the sleeve that she'd felt under her face as she was held against John Thompson's body that day in the lighthouse, and again in her bedroom when she was healing from her own wounds.

That familiar piece of clothing flooded her with all her stress and worry from the last few days. She felt lightheaded and had to reach out and steady herself with the wall by the doorway.

"What is going on?" she whispered to Catharine. "Why is John's shirt there?"

But Catharine was already out of range, outside the door, leaving her to encounter whatever this was on her own.

She stared at the figure in the bed. She saw the sheets move up and down. Whoever it was, was at least still breathing.

She moved forward hesitantly, but she felt driven by something powerful inside.

She had to know if it was him.

She had to see him.

But she was afraid of what she might find under those sheets.

She felt her legs moving, but she had no recollection of how she actually made it to his bedside.

She peeked around his body and could see his dark hair, slicked back and greasy, above bandages covering part of his face.

It was him.

Every part of her body knew it was him.

"John?" she said softly. "Oh, John."

And then she was sobbing. She felt the hot tears fall from her eyes. Relief that he was there and that he was breathing, but so much worry too.

His hand was laying on the bed next to him, on top of the sheet. She took it in hers and held it gently.

"I'm here, John. I'm so sorry I couldn't get to you sooner."

She cried thick tears that ran down her cheeks and onto his bedding. He didn't move.

One of the younger, female nurses came into the room and stood next to her silently. Charlotte searched her face with her eyes, pleading for information.

"He has a lot of injuries," the nurse finally spoke. "He is going to be here a while."

Charlotte grabbed a chair from the wall and scooted it next to the bed. "I will be here with him then, for as long as it takes."

Catharine entered the room and stood next to her, putting her hand on her shoulder and squeezing softly. "I will be here too," she assured her.

"Does Andrew know he is here?" Charlotte asked through the tears that continued to pour down her face.

"Does anyone know how badly he is injured? And why is he here? How did he get here?" She had so many questions. Nothing made sense.

"Andrew knows," Catharine said. "He was who told me to find you. You came into the hospital just in time for me to do that."

"I'm so glad you did," she said. "I need to be with him. Oh my God, I've needed him so much."

Catharine nodded. "I know."

"I will get the doctor when he is available," the nurse told them. "He can tell you what injuries Mr. Thompson has."

They both thanked the nurse, and she walked out the door.

Charlotte put her head on John's hand that she was still holding, and gently brushed his fingers with her lips.

"I'm here," she kept saying, over and over. She didn't know if he could hear her, but if he could, she wanted him to know he wasn't alone.

"Where is Aaron?" Charlotte asked Catharine. "If John is here, Aaron must be, too…?"

But Catharine shook her head. "I looked and I've asked everyone who came in with John. No one saw a

Black man on the ship."

"But how did John get on that ship? Where was that ship from?"

Catharine shrugged. "No one has explained that to me yet," she admitted.

The doctor came in eventually. He introduced himself and told them that there were severe injuries, and the patient was unlikely to make it very long.

Charlotte gasped and felt the world spinning at those words.

"It is possible that if he makes it the next night or two, and we see improvement in his burns and the injuries to his right foot, he may wake and might actually survive. But we just don't know," the doctor went on.

"What is wrong with his foot?" Charlotte asked, steadying herself, knowing that she was going to have to be John's strongest advocate at this point. He was unable to ask these questions, and someone had to make sure that less harm than good came from this frontier medical care.

"And why is he so burned?" she continued.

"Ma'am," the doctor sighed, "it appears he has

been in some kind of tragic explosion or fire. His foot has had sections torn completely away, and his skin is marked with horrible burns all over his body."

The explosion…

Charlotte tried to stay strong. This was awful information. He could not be dying. Especially when she finally just found him again.

She ground her teeth together to keep herself steady. "What can we do?"

The doctor shrugged, "At this point we just have to wait and see how he heals. I've given him some powerful narcotics to keep him asleep. It appears the fire also cauterized his foot wounds, so either the infection will overcome him quickly or his body may have a fighting chance. We just won't know until he either wakes or perishes. I am very sorry."

Charlotte rubbed John's hand softly and tears started to fall again. True medical knowledge was hard to come by those days, but especially in a distant town like Key West. She was just thankful John was in a clean facility and that people were there to care for him the best they could.

She understood the waiting game, but it was going

to be torturous to wait so long. She needed him to wake up. She needed to know he was okay. And she needed to find out where Aaron was.

She sat back in the chair and was determined to stay until he woke up, no matter how long that took.

Charlotte spent a lot of time sitting in the hospital over the next few weeks. Andrew and Catharine were wonderful- bringing her food and drink and taking turns sitting with him while she took breaks to relieve herself. They brought in a cot for her to sleep next to his bed so she could be there as much as possible.

She refused to leave his side and asked a lot of questions whenever anyone came to change his bandages or turn his body to prevent sores.

Staying there meant she also missed out on going on the wrecking ship. She was torn about missing the opportunity to go see if Aaron was still at the light station. But she figured if he was still there after all these weeks, he must be okay enough to wait while John recovered. Otherwise, it had been so long that he was either somewhere else, or… Charlotte had to admit to herself: it was possible he was no longer alive.

Either way, John had to take priority.

She had to try not to think about Aaron for a while as she sat with John. He had to recover. He could tell her where to find Aaron. He could explain what happened. But only if he survived.

Day in and day out she was there to watch him breathe. And luckily, he kept doing so.

After about three more weeks, Charlotte noticed him move his fingers a little bit. She told the doctor, and they stopped giving him so much medication so he could perhaps start waking up more naturally.

His burns had mostly healed, and his foot was showing signs of new skin growth on the broken areas.

After a week of changing bandages, the doctor said he was pleased to see that although John would likely never use that foot again, the risk of gangrene had gone down. Apparently, whatever burned his body had also stopped the injury from rotting.

So, the doctor told them that he was not going to die of disease or infection at that point, but they still didn't know if he would wake. The narcotics they used were new and they weren't sure if the dose would allow him to ever wake up.

But eventually he did.

Charlotte was at his side when his eyes started to open. She felt him wiggle a little in the bed next to her, where she was still holding his hand as often as possible so he could feel her touch and maybe know he wasn't alone.

"John?" she cried out, "are you awake?!"

She put her head closer to his and watched as his eyelid fluttered. And then he squinted, opening his eyes just slightly. She could hear him moaning softly.

"Sit still, John," she urged, "I will go get someone to help you."

He shook his head and she saw him mouth the word "no."

"Okay," she said, "I will stay right here with you. Do you need anything?"

He seemed to make a swallowing motion.

"A drink?" she asked. He carefully nodded.

He must be so thirsty, she thought. She knew they had given him some shots of fluids over the last few weeks and tried to help him swallow some water they gave him with syringes in his mouth. But he had not had an actual drink of fluid other than those efforts since who knew when.

She ran to the doorway and told one of the volunteers who was circulating to tell the doctor that John was awake and that he needed something to drink.

The woman ran down the hall and came back quickly with a cup of water. "I am going to find the doctor now," she promised, and was back out the door.

Charlotte helped John take a drink, easing his head up and tilting the glass.

Once he drank a little, he smiled at her. "Oh, Charlotte," he whispered. "Where are we?"

"Shhh," she tried to hush him. "Save your strength. I'm so glad you're awake. We are in Key West at a hospital."

He continued anyway, "Oh, Charlotte. Key West…. Oh, I've missed you so much. I was so sure the Seminole had killed you too."

"No, I'm here. I'm okay," she said. "No one is killed."

She watched John's face turn dark and he sighed deeply and then started coughing for a minute.

"That's not true Charlotte," he paused. "Aaron is gone," he reached for her hand that she pulled back from him at those words. "I tried to help him. But he is gone."

"What?" Charlotte called out in the echoing room.

"What do you mean, gone?" she shouted again, even more loudly, "what do you mean? He left? Where did he go?"

She felt her head reeling while her heart knew exactly what John was trying to tell her.

"I'm sorry, Charlotte. I tried," he stuttered. But then he seemed to get a burst of energy. "I have to tell you. You need to know."

Charlotte tried to quiet him down so he wouldn't say such awful things. She was afraid to know. But she couldn't stop him.

He kept talking.

"The Seminole shot at us, and he was fatally shot. We didn't know it at first. He made it up inside the lighthouse and we hoped we would be able to survive. But then they lit the lighthouse on fire to try to smoke us out. We couldn't breathe. It was Aaron's idea to light the gunpowder to kill us faster. The fire was so hot. We were choking on the smoke. We didn't want to burn slowly. So, we threw one of the kegs of powder down into the fire. We thought it would collapse the tower. But it didn't. It actually stopped the fire."

Charlotte was shaking her head and her whole body was shaking at that point. The explosion. She remembered seeing the flames and hearing and feeling the bang. But she didn't know what had really happened. She had so hoped that they had made it out and the explosion happened after they were safely away from danger.

"Did the explosion kill Aaron?" she asked, not wanting to understand but starting to realize what terror John had experienced in that tower while she was being whisked away by the Natives.

"No," he said softly. "No. It was the gunshot wound. It hit him in the back. I got hit in my foot, and then the explosion somehow blew up around our legs too. I thought I would die from the injuries from that. But Aaron was already gone. He bled out while I was throwing the gunpowder. I never heard him talk again."

Charlotte was sobbing now. Big, thick tears were pounding down on her blouse, and she was wiping her face with her hands.

"Oh, Aaron," she cried out. "Oh, my Aaron."

She couldn't imagine the world without her best

friend. All this time she had grasped firmly to the idea that she would indeed see him again.

But she would never get to do that now.

Images of his sweet face and the way he always looked deeply into her eyes flashed in her mind. She gasped for air as this new reality gripped her.

"I'm sorry, Charlotte," John winced as he moved towards her to try to comfort her.

Just then, the doctor rounded the doorway. He stared at her face and was taken aback. "Oh, is something happening that I need to know about? I was told that Mr. Thompson woke up. Is there something wrong?"

Charlotte managed to stop crying for a minute. "No, Doctor. I'm sorry. I'm very glad that John is awake. I just heard news that our other friend is gone."

The doctor nodded briskly at the situation and then rushed to John's side, obviously not interested in engaging in the sad situation but wanting to stay on-task to make sure his patient was checked out well. He checked John's pulse in his wrist and felt his forehead, then asked him to show him some of the bandages to make sure they were not soiled and that they were still in place.

Charlotte took the opportunity of this new distraction to wipe her eyes and her face and to attempt to compose herself. The whole thing was a very bad dream. John was injured badly enough, and now she knew that Aaron had died… so much more than she wanted to deal with ever. And yet, she was still breathing. And John was breathing and awake. Which was a much better outcome than if she'd lost him too.

She watched as the doctor checked John's wounds and then left the room. Then John motioned to her to come closer, and he pulled her into his arms.

"I'm not able to be very strong for you yet, Charlotte," he whispered. "But I will never leave you again. Ever."

She nodded and leaned into his grip. "I am so sorry you went through so much," she told him. She could only imagine how terrified he must have been.

"I laid in that tower for days, thinking I would never see you again… that I would never hold you again…" he said, his voice wavering.

"They took me away into the Everglades on horses and I didn't even know where I was," Charlotte explained. "They were going to kill me, but they didn't. Mica was there and she talked them into letting me stay alive and then she helped me leave…"

She tried to summarize the whole ordeal into one breath. But there was so much to explain. They would need to let John heal first, and then they could talk more.

"But how did you end up on the shipwreck ship… I think they called it the *Maria*…?" she asked, realizing that part didn't make any sense.

"The explosion was so loud that the crew of the *U.S.S. Motto*, an Army ship, heard it twelve miles out to sea," he started to explain.

Charlotte gasped. "Wow, you're so lucky you did that explosion. How else would anyone know to come check on the light station? What if no one had heard anything?" She shuddered at the alternative.

He nodded carefully. "They came and they found me. I think I was pretty close to dying. I was having weird dreams. They took me out to sea to try to take me somewhere safer. They ended up crossing paths with the *Maria* and that ship had a doctor on board. So, they transferred me to the ship so they could continue on their way and not worry with me. The doctor gave me some strong narcotics. The next thing I knew I was here, with you."

She nodded, hushing him as she cradled his wounded chest in her arms. "I'm so glad they found you," she said.

They held each other for what seemed like seconds but ended up being days.

Charlotte refused to leave the room except to use the facilities and John continued to gain strength every day.

Every chance they had they were holding each other. John's wounds were healing well, and he was finally able to stand up and try to walk. It was a new situation, with him only regaining a partial use of his mangled foot, but he was determined to walk again. And Charlotte was there to cheer him on every day.

Andrew and Catharine told her to not worry about anything else for a while. They were making decent money with the mapmaking and other services for all of the people flooding down to the Keys. The Indian War was in full swing, so shiploads of Americans flocked down to Key West. It was known as one of the safeholds that had never been attacked. Its isolated location lent itself well to military blockades along the new roads, and the Seminole seemed to prefer attacks on areas where they could more easily slip back into the Everglades.

Charlotte sometimes heard bits and pieces of the news. She wondered if Mica was doing okay. But she also hoped she never had to see her or her tribemates again. As much as she felt loyal to her friend in the past, she was beyond worrying about much other than John right now. And Mica's people had taken her away so that she wasn't able to help John and Aaron… she would never forgive them for that.

At night when John slept, Charlotte fought with her own demons. She wondered what she could have done to prevent them from being ambushed by the Seminole that tragic day at the light station. She wondered if she had just not insisted on them worrying about the light staying lit, if they could have made it to Key West all together. Perhaps she could have led them away from danger, instead of forcing them all to go to the station.

And there were so many memories of the good times with Aaron playing through her mind. The way Aaron insisted on staying and helping her with the light, even when he could have gone straight to the Bahamas

when Andrew left. And his loyalty that got him killed…
She felt like the accomplice, or even the complete cause
of him being gone. It was killing her inside.

But day after day, John held her as he healed. She lived for those moments when felt his skin next to hers. He was still covered in bandages and had to move carefully, but when no one was around he would motion for her to sneak over and crawl under his covers with him. They listened to each other's heartbeats and felt the warmth of each other's bodies.

It was going to be a long winter with a lot of healing time, but Charlotte was oblivious to just about everything and everyone except for John Thompson.

Chapter Twenty-Five

It was silent when they walked through the front gate at the light station several months later.

Not even birds were singing today. The clouds parted and the ground was permeated with the sweet and dank smells of wet moss and rotting leaves where the rains had soaked it.

They avoided the puddles as they walked towards the keeper's cottage.

None of them spoke as they looked around at the broken structure and the charred lumber that once held their lives inside.

Charlotte picked up a lone pot that the Natives must have either dropped or tossed out while looking to see what, if anything was left unburned. She held it in her hands and turned it as she walked towards the light tower.

The broken tower structure was all that remained. Everything else was gone.

Andrew put his hand on her shoulder as she turned to him with wide eyes. "I'm sorry, Charlotte," he whispered.

John gripped Charlotte's hand in his and she could feel his pulse in his fingertips.

They had to see for themselves what was left. To know if there was anything worth trying to save. And to remember…

Charlotte still wanted to believe they could return and find Aaron. She looked to the broken-out windows of the keepers' cottage and imagined how it would have been if he was standing in the window waving to them. If the house was already fixed up, because that was what Aaron would have done if he had been left there. She imagined what it would be like if the grounds were manicured and beautiful like he always kept them. And what an amazing reunion they were supposed to be having.

But he was not there. His absence was screaming at them from every corner of the property.

She looked at the light tower and remembered how

many times she had climbed those stairs and delicately caressed each panel of glass in those windows and each piece of the Fresnel lens for years and years. The top of the tower was still standing, jutting out into the clearing like a broken vase. The bottom was seared with ashes and soot from the fire. The top was missing all the glass from the explosion.

Charlotte winced as she glimpsed the top of the tower and imagined how it must have felt to be John and Aaron, with fire raging all around them and the stairs all burned out. No way to get down, and cooking above the flames.

She was so thankful that John was rescued.

They still hadn't had an opportunity to find out who specifically on the *U.S.S. Motto* had made the call to sail closer to shore to check on the explosion. She imagined John was on his last breaths when he called out to the crew as they came ashore, and he heard them talking. She was so thankful for all of them.

Andrew kept shaking his head. The reality of what they had all gone through was breaking his heart. He continued saying over and over again how sorry he was that he'd left them there.

"It isn't your fault," Charlotte said, hugging her brother tightly.

They both had so many tears still, even after all of this time. "I wanted to stay here when you all left to Key West. I wanted to make sure Mica and her family were okay. I just didn't know it would mean losing so much."

He nodded.

John put his hands on each of their shoulders. "It is hard being back here," he said. "I keep remembering that horrible day and night, and the others after that when I was stuck and hurting. But what I really remember most is how awful it felt to hear Charlotte yelling when the Seminole captured her…" his voice drifted off.

Andrew nodded and took John's hand in his. "I know you would have tried to get to her if it was at all possible," he said.

"I would have moved heaven and earth to get to her," he agreed. "So would Aaron…" he added.

They all looked out at the beautiful ocean waters, lapping against the shore just beyond the light tower.

"Aaron would be glad we found each other again," Charlotte said softly.

John and Andrew both nodded their heads.

"I will never forget his loyalty and friendship," Andrew said.

"And his big smile," Charlotte said, tears falling on her cheeks as she smiled just thinking of his beautiful face.

"And his bravery," John added.

They all stood, faces to the bright sun, thinking about their dear friend.

Then they turned and walked away, leaving everything behind them and heading into the future where they hoped they could eventually live in a world without the Indian Wars, without the need for a Saltwater Underground Railroad, and without the divisions that people create that lead to such nightmare situations.

They walked back down the driveway and joined up with the others who were waiting for them to return to the wrecker ship so they could go back to their new lives in Key West.

Charlotte could have sworn she saw something flash from the top of the light tower as their ship pulled away from shore and she caught one last glimpse of the tip of Cape Florida.

About the Author

Kathleen Casper is an educator and an attorney who has lived in the Tampa Bay Area of Florida and the Pacific Northwest. After falling in love with lighthouses and maritime history, she began "collecting" lighthouses by visiting as many as she could find, all along the coasts of America, and then worldwide. She enjoys kayaking, spending time with her family and pets, and traveling the globe.

Kathleen is also the author of the following books:

Keeper of the Cape: Cape Arago

Smart Babies: A guide for identifying and supporting gifted traits in infants and young children

How Do I go on Without You? A Journal of Love for Those Who Have Lost

She also authored other articles on education and life, including many you can find on the http://OneWorldGifted.weebly.com blog.

Made in the USA
Middletown, DE
29 October 2022